FLY
Dancing with Gravity
Part II

By Doc Skinner

FLY
Dancing With Gravity
Part II

by

Doc Skinner

There are too many to thank for supporting me during this adventure. Remember, as long as we ALL lift each other, we will ALL rise together... Also know that funds from the sale of these books will go toward producing these stories as a film. If you would like to get more involved in Film Production or just contact the author for interviews, please email docskinner@gmail.com. I appreciate your support. Now, on with the story.

-Doc Skinner

1028 Publishing House © 2025

<u>TABLE OF CONTENTS</u>

1028 Publishing House © 2025

1028 Publishing House © 2025

Chapter 1

<u>DEVISING THE PLAN</u>

It's a beautiful day in the Spanish coastal town of Empuriabrava, Spain, where we see a towering building at the end of a small airport runway. The name "Windoor" is on the top of the building. This is the location and event where dreams come true once a year in January. This is the Wind Games, where the best of the best in indoor skydiving come to compete. It is their form of the Olympics for indoor skydiving. For years, flyers and fans tried to get indoor skydiving into the Olympics. Even 3-time World Champion and professional instructor Leonid Volkov made a beautiful, inspiring, and compelling video to be sent to the Olympic committee. The hope was to bring Indoor Skydiving to the forefront on the world stage. Unfortunately, do to technicalities, indoor skydiving was taken off the list, and break dancing and Skateboarding became the new Olympic sports in 2024. Break dancing...hmm.. Well, we all saw how that turned out, didn't we?

From outside the building, amongst the Spanish coastal skyline, we hear muffled music and people cheering. Music is thumping as we walk through a doorway to a staircase that ascends to the second floor. There are people of all ages and nationalities filling the room, show reporters televising the event live around the world, displaying talented Indoor Flyers within the air chamber in the center of the room. The crowd cheered for each contestant as they performed their art of Body Flight.

In the lounge area downstairs, Leonid Volkov, and his partner Dmitriy are finishing their sandwiches before Leonid's competition. American rock music is playing in the background as Leonid watches competition videos on his laptop. Dmitriy says to Leonid, "It's Time." Leonid closes his laptop and responds, "Dah."

Leonid Volkov walks out, and the crowd goes nuts. The music segment begins. Leonid, like the performer he is, stands still, his head bowed in his helmet. The music hits a downbeat, and Leonid begins a choreographed dance as he walks toward the chamber entrance. On the next big downbeat,

Leonid launches up in the chamber and proceeds to a stunning performance with unbeatable skill and control. The crowd continues cheering him on as a local podcaster streams the event on her iPhone. We see her perspective through the phone and zoom out to the same footage on Jett Parker's TV Screen in his living room, back in the United States, in Pinetop-Lakeside, Arizona.

Jett Parker, now seventeen and a senior at Blueridge High School, along with his teammates, The Wind Flyers, are sitting around watching the Competition live in the living room. Jett says, "I think it's time, guys. It's been two years since the last big competition. We need to go to the Wind Games and show them what we've got. We're Seniors now! Covid put a huge dent in everything and now we gotta play catch-up." Jett's Girlfriend Skyler Jenkins speaks up, "Sounds great and all but it isn't cheap to go, especially for an entire team." Bodhi jumps in with his two cents of knowledge, "You have to pay for flights, hotels, trains, and cab fares." Draven Pierce does the same, "Don't forget food, can't forget the food, I've been told the food is amazing in Spain." Zoe

McAdams pipes in with the important stuff, "And the most important and not cheap is the visas and passports. We would all need to get them." At that moment, Jett's Mom, Annie Parker, walks into the living room with snacks and responds, as most parents would, "That does sound pretty expensive," she says. Jett replies, "Come on, it's just another challenge. God knows we have survived many challenges over the past two years. But aren't you ready to get back to competing? We proved to the mountain how good we are, so let's show the world!"

Lilly Parker, Jett's little sister and the biggest brainiac in the room, reminds everyone of the cold, hard facts. "I hate to be the bearer of bad news, Jett, but the next Wind Games is after you graduate. This was the last one before you graduate, and some of you will be off to college." Bodhi Thatcher with disappointment says, "Oh, snap! Lilly's right. The pandemic really screwed us." Logan Fletcher speaks up, "We missed out on so much. I'm glad we get to at least graduate." Skyler like a born leader, speaks up with encouragement, "Now, hold on, guys. The Wind

Games aren't the only competition in the world." Lilly pulls out her laptop and says, "I'll check for all the competitions between now and the end of the school year." With renewed hope, Bodhi responds with an overzealous "Sweet." Skyler, with a glimmer in her eyes, tells the team, "Before I was born, my mom used to go to competitions around the world. She said, if I ever got the opportunity to travel, I should take it, so I'm down!." Everyone in the room takes turns looking at each other. Annie Parker looks at Jett and smiles. Jett says, "I say we talk to Coach tomorrow after school." The entire team agreed and started to get excited about the idea.

Chapter 2

<u>MISSIONS A GO</u>

It's another beautiful day in the White Mountains of Arizona. The sun is shining, and the music is pumping. Bhodi and Jett are pulling into the school parking lot as the song comes to an end, when we hear the Morning & Evening DJ, Dan "The Man" Dravenski, a Local Pillar in the community. "Another beautiful morning here in the White Mountains. Today we will have a high of 82 and a low of 63, partly cloudy skies with wind gusts up to fifteen miles per hour. Speaking of wind, the owners of iFly, the McAdams, are doing a special family discount this weekend for all locals. So, come on out and catch some air. Here is a little ditty to pump up your day." Dan "The Man" Dravenski plays a thumping tune.

Jett turns off the radio and says to Bodhi, "I know we can pull this off. We just need support." Bodhi replies, "I'll talk to my mom, who can talk to Principal Wallace." Jett responds, "Ok, but let's talk to coach first." "Cool," Bodhi says.

Jett and Bodhi walk down the halls of Blueridge High School, home of the Yellowjackets. We see signs being hung on the

1028 Publishing House © 2025

walls with the colors purple and gold for FUTURE CAREER DAY. Lilly walks up and joins them. "So, I found a bunch of competitions online last night. I think we can make this happen." She says. Bodhi, with a look of excitement, replies, "I'm getting so pumped!" But he abruptly stops when the group approaches Principal Wallace. With kindness but from an authoritative position, Principal Wallace acknowledges the kids. "Good morning, kids!" Jett replies first, "Good Morning, Principal Wallace." Bodhi replies, "Good Morning, Sir." Lilly follows with her confident smile, "Morning!" Principal Wallace looks at all of them and asks a question. "You three seem very cheerful this morning. Are you excited about Future Career Day?" he hands them all Flyers. Jett with Curiosity asks Principal Wallace, "What's the difference between the normal Career Day and Future Career Day?" Principal Wallace Smiles and replies, "Well, I am so glad you asked. Future Career Day is about careers that are literally out of this world!" Bodhi's eyes widen, and he asks, "Like in space?" With a chuckle, Principal Wallace responds, "Exactly, Mr. Thatcher, Space jobs off planet." Lilly jumps in, "So by the time I graduate, I can work in space?" She asks Principal Wallace. He replies, "Indeed, Ms. Parker." Jett's eyes grow wide as he looks over the flyer and sees the Planetary Defense logo. "Planetary Defense will be here?" Jett Asks. "Yes, Mr. Parker, they will have a representative here that day to recruit." Principal Wallace replies. Jett and the kids are stunned. Jett asks for affirmation that he understood correctly, "Recruit? Like, go into Planetary Defense?" Like a proud father, Principal Wallace responds, "Anyone who is 18 or about to turn 18 by the end of the school year is eligible." Bodhi energetically replies, "Oh man, this is cool!" Principal Wallace looks at his watch and says, "So don't be late and miss something. It could change your life. But for now, get to class." The kids hurry off to class.

1028 Publishing House © 2025

Chapter 3

<u>HELD TO HIGHER STANDARDS</u>

Mrs. Kathy Thatcher, Bodhi's Mom, is teaching a class and writing something on the marker board. Bodhi, Jett, and Skyler are whispering in the back of the class. Mrs. Thatcher turns to catch them and calls out, "Bodhi Nathaniel Thatcher!" The students respond with oohs and laughter. One of the students says, "Nathaniel's in trouble!" with a look of embarrassment and shame, and snaps back at the student, "Shut up, dude!" His mother Chimes in, "That's enough, everyone." Mrs. Thatcher gives Bodhi a stern look, and Bodhi looks away, embarrassed. Jett leans into Bodhi and whispers, "Sorry, Brother." At that moment, the bell rings, and the class gathers their things and heads out of class. Bodhi tries to sneak past his mom to no avail. She stops him in his tracks. "Bodhi?" Bodhi freezes as Skyler, Jett, and the other students go by. Jett empathetically says, "Good Luck." Skyler follows up with, "See you after school." Bodhi, with his head down, replies, "Maybe."

The last student walks out of the classroom, then Mrs. Thatcher speaks, "Bodhi, come on. I know it's rough having your mom as a teacher. But

1028 Publishing House © 2025

it makes it that much more important that you are a shining example to other students. And I mean by paying attention in class, for one." Bodhi, looking down, responds, "Sorry, Mom, I'm just really excited about something." "And what would that be?" she says. He replies, "That's Classified." Sternly looking at her son, she says, "Bhodie." Bodhi says to her, "For now at least, gotta talk to coach first." With a stern voice, Mrs. Thatcher tells Bodhi, "Get to class!" Bodhi responds while walking away, "Yes, Ma'am."

1028 Publishing House © 2025

Chapter 4

<u>HAVING WHAT IT TAKES</u>

We see Annie Parker behind the counter, talking flirtatiously with the facility owner, Tanner McAdams. The kids all walk in and see the encounter. The girls see it as sweet, and the boys see it as a chance to tease Jett about it as they walk up to the couple. Bodhi whispers to Jett, "Think you'll have to change your name to Jett McAdams?" Bodhi and Draven snicker. Jett firmly responds, "That's never going to happen." Skyler jumps in, "I think it's beautiful that your mom and Coach found each other. Just like we found each other." Zoe throws into the conversation, "I think Jett's freaked out he may have two sisters one day." Jett is not enthused as they reach the counter. "Hey, kids!" Annie says, "I just wanted to stop by and see this amazing man before I head to work." Annie grabs Tanner's face, squishes it, and plants a big kiss on him. Jett begins to squirm in his own skin, "Mom, come on! Time and place, gee." Annie, blushing, says, "You kids have fun." Annie looks at Coach McAdams with a flirty eye and says, "I'll see you later, Mr. Man of mine." Annie Parker walks out, and the kids are doing their best not to bust out in laughter. Coach McAdams is turning red, and Jett

1028 Publishing House © 2025

looks uncomfortable. Lilly, Zoe, and Skyler start to giggle. Zoe blurts out while giggling, "Mr. Man of mine." The group loses control and starts laughing. Coach McAdams regains his composure. "Alright, Alright, get it out of your systems." He says. Skyler backs him up and says, "It's cool, coach. It's really sweet how you two are." Coach, under his breath, says, "Thanks, Skyler." He turns to the team and begins speaking, "All right, Ms. Parker clued me in on what you want to talk about. So, do you think you are ready to get on the circuit —on a global scale? OK, let's see what you got. Today will officially be the Wind Games, White Mountain style. So, you have 20 minutes to figure out which routine you are doing, suit up. You get one chance and will be judged by your fellow flyers, not your teammates." The kids seem confident and cocky. Coach McAdams continues, "So I want you to think about this hard. Think about all the long, hard hours working for the money for the expensive trip to be in a Chamber on the other side of the world and having only one shot, which is around three minutes, to make it all worthwhile while not screwing up." The kids don't look as confident as they did a few moments before. Coach McAdams continues, "So, let's see how ready you are. See you in the chamber in, now 19 minutes."

Chapter 5

HUMBLE PIE

The kids scramble to get changed and prepare for their moment. Coach Tanner McAdams goes behind the counter and grabs a microphone. "Attention all flyers, Attention all flyers. In 18 minutes, we will be having an impromptu version of our own Wind Games. Judges will be needed." Flyers throughout the building scamper around, moving seats and chairs around the glass chamber. The music begins to jam as the team prepares.

Eighteen minutes later, Coach McAdams gets back on the microphone, "This will be strictly a Solo comp between the members of the Wind Flyers. So, grab your snacks cause I have no clue what will happen... First up, Draven Pierce." The team members are all in the holding cell, cheering each other on. A new song begins, and Draven goes into the chamber. At first, he is smooth but Stumbles against the glass, causing him to fall behind in the song and miss maneuvers. Coach McAdams makes a face as he announces the next flyer, "Next up, Lilly Parker." Lilly's song starts, and Lilly goes into the chamber and does a decent job with her routine. She exits the chamber, thinking she did better than expected, only to see the replay on the screen. She sees that her legs and arms are like spaghetti, with no form, as they should have been. Coach gets back on the microphone: "Logan Fletcher." Logan walks up to the chamber door, hamming up to the crowd and getting the crowd pumped up. The music starts, and he gestures for it to be turned up. The music is blaring. Logan walks in, standing on the net, getting the crowd pumped. He jumps up and lets the air take him, then proceeds with a crowd-stomping routine until we see that one of his shoes isn't tied and is loose. The wind is trying to take it, and Logan realizes he is about to lose his shoe, so he tries to fix it, stopping his performance. The crowd looks and sounds deflated for the flyer. Logan steps out of the chamber, upset. Coach is back on the microphone: "Next up, Zoe McAdams." Zoe's Music starts to play, a mellow yet beautiful piece. Zoe performs a beautiful Routine and receives high scores. We hear the coach over the system: "Next up, Bodhi Thatcher." Bodhi comes out strong, hitting every mark till he comes down fast and hard with a pinwheel spin, and his heel catches the chamber door opening, spinning him in the opposite direction, making him crash into the glass. The crowd reacts with a loud "Ooh!" Bodhi keeps going and finishes his routine, and the crowd cheers. Coach announces, "Skyler

Jenkins." As only Skyler would do, in her all-white suit and helmet at the chamber door, she cues the music. She slowly falls in and, like an angel, levitates to the very top of the chamber, slowly gliding down to the crowd, doing a beautifully choreographed routine. When she finishes, she does a slow back roll out the door. The crowd gets to its feet, cheering. Skyler waves to everyone. The Judges give a high score.

Coach comments, then announces Jett, "Great job, Skyler. And finally, Jett Parker." Jett, after seeing his teammates falter, felt his confidence was quickly diminishing. With worry in his eyes, Jett waves to the crowd and the judges and cues his music. At that moment, all of his moves were playing out at once in his head, not out of order, but all at once. He panicked and froze. Skyler is outside the chamber, gesturing to him to go! Jett dives into the chamber and goes all impromptu. He does a bunch of random moves. Coach Tanner McAdam shakes his head. The judges raised their scorecards, and Jett got low numbers.

The team and Coach Tanner McAdams are sitting in the practice area after their Impromptu Wind Games Competition. The Team looks deflated. Coach speaks up first, " Still, feel like

1028 Publishing House © 2025

you are ready?" The team is dismayed. Coach Adams begins his critique while looking at his notes. "If you have never had Humbled Pie, you will now. Draven, the simplest mistakes can cost you a lot of time. With just one miscalculated move, you were off the rest of your routine by 3 seconds. Lilly, we have a lot of work to do on your posture and form. Logan, a simple wardrobe malfunction due to laziness and a lack of pride in your outfit. Bodhi, arrogance will get you nowhere. Entertaining the crowd is great and all, but when it gets in the way of your routine, it's time to re-evaluate. Skyler and Zoe, there is always room to improve, but your routines were worthy today because you both practice every day, but don't let it get to your head. And Jett, what happened? That wasn't even a routine. That was you free frolicking in the air chamber all willy-nilly." Coach Tanner McAdams is starting to turn a little red, get a little sweaty, and get a little dizzy. Zoe, with concern, asks, "Dad, are you ok?" He responds with a smirk, "Yeah, I'm fine. I just got a little lightheaded." The team looks a little concerned. Trying to reassure them, he says, "I'm fine, really. But do you see the point I'm trying to make here? For us to do a huge trip for a brief moment in time, we must be sure that we are ready and not waste a lot of time and money for nothing." The team looks hopeless, and the coach sees it. He continues, "But that does not mean it's not worth it, let alone impossible." Anyway, first things first, we need to figure out where we want to compete and how much it will cost, then make sure everyone gets their passports. Once that's done, it's time to train and raise the funds at school functions, car washes, bake sales, and yard work. Whatever we can do to raise the money. The most important thing out of everything is Training, Training, Training, Training, and then some more training. Now, are you guys ready for this?" The team, in unison, says, "Yes!" Coach continues, "For some of you, this is your Senior year, so let's make it memorable." The team and Coach McAdams put their hands in the middle and, in unison, yell, "WIND FLYERS!"

Outside the iFly, the kids get in their cars to head out, and we hear Dan "The Man" Dravenski come on the car stereo. "This just in! Local Champs, Team Wind Flyers from Blue Ridge High School, are raising money to compete against the world's best overseas, and they need your help. Wind Flyers, this song is for you. Good luck and put me down for $20." The kids are stunned. Skyler speaks first, "How did he?" Jett jumps in, "We just decided this an hour ago." The kids looked at each other, puzzled, questioning how he knew this already. Another song blasts out of the speakers, and the kids drive away.

Chapter 6

<u>FUNDRAISING</u>

The halls of Blueridge High School are buzzing as students head to lunch. Zoe has a jar full of change and cash and is trying to get every dollar she can from fellow students as she walks down the hall. "Come on, everyone, every little bit counts. Remember, we're not just representing our school but THE UNITED STATES OF AMERICA. It's your patriotic duty." She announces. Another outcast named Charlie speaks his mind, "Seriously? Pulling the Patriot card?" Zoe responds with a smile, "When you see us on TV representing our country, you will be proud you did your part." The boy fluffs his lip as Zoe bashes her eyes at him. And like most boys at that age, when a woman smiled at you, you melted. Charlie submits and grabs his wallet, "Fine! Put me down for..." Charlie riffles through his wallet and pulls out a Twenty-dollar Bill. Sadly, he says, "Sorry, all I have is a." Zoe grabs the twenty-dollar bill and says, "A twenty? That's ok, Every little bit counts, no matter how big or small." Zoe smiles at Charlie, and Charlie's frown goes to a forced smile. Like a sad puppy, he says quietly, "Right, not like that was my beer money or anything." Zoe responds,

"Oh, Charlie, not only have you shown true patriotism, but you allowed me to save your life tonight by not having your beer and ending up in the hospital or worse. Plus, if no one told you, twenty-one is the age to drink, and anyone like that isn't someone in whom I would show interest. Would I?" Poor Charlie looks defeated and says, "No."

Zoe walks off while having the last word, "Stick to your dreams, Charlie. I can see you being a pilot one day." Stunned, Charlie replies, "Wait? Really? A pilot?" Zoe smiles at him and says, "I hope so." Zoe smiles and walks away with the Twenty-dollar bill in the air, then plopping it in the jar.

In the Cafeteria Jett, Bodhi, Logan, and Draven are selling their team Wind Flyer shirts and collecting money when a group of three pretty girls approaches the boys. "Hi, Jett," Pixie says. The girls are more into Jett than the others. As they start to flirt with Jett, he tries his best to redirect them to his friends. The second Girl, Karen, asks, "So is it true you are raising money to go to Europe?" Jett, looking extremely uncomfortable, says, "Yes. We all are, all of us on the team," gesturing to his teammates. The third girl, Hannah, asks Jett as she slowly moves in like a cheetah ready to pounce on her prey. "So, do girlfriends get to go?" Jett gets flustered, and his eyes grow wide when, out of nowhere, Skyler appears, surprising everyone. "The only Girlfriends that get to go are the ones on the team. Are you on the team, Hannah?" She said. The three girls look at each other, speechless. Skyler continues with a fiery rage in her eyes, "No? I didn't think so... Now, as I see it, you three ladies have two choices." With a smart snarky attitude Pixie says, "Really? What would that be?" Skyler turns to Pixie, "Well, Pixie, the first choice is this. I properly introduce you to these three fine young gentlemen who would love to be your date for the prom... Think about it, you get to truly know someone and have a deeper relationship, rather than your normal selection from the shallow end of the gene pool." The boys looked flustered yet intrigued to see how this was going to play out. Karen, like a complaining snob says, "And the second choice?" Skyler looks deep into Karen's soul like the Grim Reaper, "Well, Karen, just for the safety of everyone in the vicinity, you make the smart choice and walk away because my man is not available. Clear?" The girls look at the boys and make a stink face. Skyler lunges at the girls and makes them flinch. In unison, they screech and

1028 Publishing House © 2025

run off. The boys are bummed. For a brief moment, they had hope.

Skyler tries to recoup their pride. "Listen, guys, they aren't worth your time. If it's any consolation, we get this money, and you will be surrounded by a higher class of ladies in Europe you can brag about, who are amazing! And you know how I know they're amazing?" Bodhi almost pouting says, "How?" Because there are female flyers, and all female flyers are amazing."

Zoe comes over and slaps down a jar filled with cash. "I think I may need a bodyguard with all this cash. What did I miss?" Skyler replies, "I was just explaining to the boys' facts that they were not privy to." With a smile Zoe says, "And what would that be?" Skyler responds, "That women are the true Bad Asses in body flight." Zoe immediately confirms, "Oh yea! Absolutely, scientifically, and indisputably proven. It's written in stone somewhere." Jett Chimes in, "That's fine, whatever you say. But Zoe, one thing I can agree on is that it's a lot of money. Good job! But we are going to need a lot more if we are going to raise $20,000."

Logan is looking through a magazine and sees an ad for an indoor flyer with a new helmet sponsor. He speaks up, "What about sponsors?"

Bodhi looks up with a grin and says, "Ah ha! Logan, I think you got something." The team's eyes light up. Jett takes the lead, "Ok, let's see, what do we need?" Skyler responds, "We need airfare, hotels, train & cab fares, and food."

Draven throws his hat into the ring, "My Uncle works for the airlines." The team is getting excited, and Jett says, "That's good, that's good. Who else do we know?" Zoe speaks up, "I can go on our fan page and make a post asking if anyone has connections to hotel chains and see if we can get any rooms. I'll talk to my dad about sponsorships for our gear, too." Skyler and Jett catch each other's eyes and smile. Skyler's lips say in silence, "I love you," and Jett's smile gets brighter. The lunch bell rings, and the kids head back to class.

1028 Publishing House © 2025

Chapter 7

<u>GUARDIAN ANGEL</u>

Inside the mysterious black jet owned by Flyer X, we see Flyer X from the waist up looking at his laptop. He is watching a YouTube fundraising video for the Wind Flyers team.

The video starts with Logan, "What's up, everybody? Logan Fletcher here, with my awesome teammates, Lilly Parker, Zoe McAdams, Skyler Jenkins, Bodhi Thatcher, Draven Pierce, and Jett Parker. We are looking for sponsors or donors to help us compete against the best in the world, representing the United States in Europe this year." Zoe jumps in, "But we can't do it without help from family, friends." Jett is now front and center on the screen and finishes the sentence, "And especially you." Skyler is next: "You can support our efforts by donating to our crowdfunding campaign site at the web address below." And last, we see Lilly saying, "And anyone who donates $40 or more gets an Official Wind Flyers Shirt."

We see Flyer X typing in a chat room with another mysterious character named Orbital. Flyer X is typing, "The team is raising money to do a European tour. What would you like me to do?" The icon blinks for a few seconds, and then text from Orbital appears: "Keep tabs and keep me informed." Flyer X closes the chat window. A second window comes up. It's the team's crowdfunding page. In the amount section, he enters $1,000, then deletes it and replaces it with $5,000. The cursor goes to the next line, which is the "From Whom" line. He ponders deciding what to put. After a moment, he signs it, Anonymous, and in the memo, writes, "Your only limitations are those that you allow. You are your own creation. Fly Fast, Fly Hard." Flyer X hits submit on the Donation button and closes the laptop.

The team is hanging out in the gym after school, sitting in the bleachers, and watching basketball practice. Lilly is doing homework, and Skyler and Zoe are adding up donations with their calculator. Skyler says, "Ok, this is what we got so far. With the help of Draven's uncle with the airline, we got our tickets, which saved us almost $10,000, all in exchange for some promo pics at the games." Bodhi turns to Draven and says, "Thank you, Brother." Draven smiles. Skyler continues, "And we still don't have hotels situated yet, and that's still a pretty penny. So far, we have raised $2,810.42. Who was the last to check the crowdfunding page?" Everyone looks at each other, saying with a look, not me!

Jett speaks up, "Zoe, check the crowdfunding page, please." Zoe pulls up the crowdfunding page. Scanning the small donations, she comes to the anonymous donor. Zoe's eyes freeze in shock, and they can't budge from looking at the number. Perplexed, Skyler asks, "Zoe, what's wrong?... Zoe?" Logan starts to panic, "Crap, did someone hack the page and steal our money?" Logan jumps up and takes the laptop, and Zoe is still frozen. Logan looks at the screen in disbelief, "Is this right?" Zoe slowly nods her head. Draven is upset, "Did we get screwed?" Jett gets louder; someone says something!" Logan breaks the silence, "An anonymous donor donated..." Logan pauses, then Zoe finishes for him, "$5,000!" The team is frozen in shock, then slowly starts to smile and grin. When all at once, they all jump up and start whooping and hollering. It was at that moment that a Basketball player passed the ball, and the noise distracted both teams, and the receiving player got smacked in the face with the basketball. Jett notices the player gets hit in the face and cringes. Jett shouts, "Sorry!" The team lowers its volume, and the basketball coach gives them a dirty look. They quickly leave the Gym.

Chapter 8

<u>102.8 FM TO THE RESCUE</u>

Inside the local pizza restaurant, we hear music playing over the restaurant speakers. A piping hot pizza is brought to the table. "Two hot, delicious, extra-large pizzas." The waiter says. Bodhi replies, "I'm starving." "Me too," Zoe replies. The kids dig into the pizza. Skyler says, "We are almost to our goal... How can we raise the rest before next week?"

At that moment, we hear Dan "The Man" Dravenski on the speakers, "That was another smash hit heard here on 102.8 FM, the White Mountains Hit station. This is Dan the Man Dravenski, letting you know that I'm here for you, the community. And when I heard local kids were raising money to compete overseas, I had to slap down a $20 bill. So tonight, let's do this show like a telethon to support our local youth. I will add another $100 to the pot. Who is with me?"

The kids are stunned. How could this be? Jett looks at the team and says, "You know what I'm thinking?" Lilly replies, "We should go to the station?" with a confident smile. Jett says, "Yep!"

1028 Publishing House © 2025

The kids slap down the money for the pizza, grab their slices, and leave quickly for their cars.

Inside Bodhi's car, the radio is playing another bomb track as Bodhi drives quickly but safely with turn signals toward the radio station. The others in the car, Jett, Draven, and Logan, are trying to call the station to let Dan the Man Dravenski know they're coming. Skyler is driving behind him with Zoe and Lilly. Bodhi asks, "Is anyone getting through?" Jett responds, "We're trying, Brother. Just keep your eyes on the road." "Copy that!" replies Bodhi.

Zoe is in Skyler's car behind the boys and gets aggravated, "Are they for real? I thought boys liked to drive fast." Music blares on the radio, an anthem that gets the kids excited.

In the quiet parking lot of 102.8 FM, we see Bodhi and Skyler's cars pull up to the radio station, and their music blares from their cars. The cars go silent as they turn off their engines, and the kids pile out. They run up to the radio station doors to find they are locked. Aggravated, Bodhi says, "Oh, come on, man!" Skyler points out to Logan that there is an intercom system on the wall behind him. "Move," she says. Skyler moves Logan aside and pushes the talk button.

Inside a dimly lit radio station, Dan "The Man" Dravenski is taking a song request over the phone. We see all twenty-eight phone lines are blinking. We hear Dan on the phone with a caller, "Yes, Ma'am, I got it, it is a great hit, and you, ma'am, are a musical muse that I cannot deny. If I can find it, then it will be next." Dan hangs up the phone. "Laurence Welk? Seriously?" The door buzzer flashes red in the Radio booth, notifying Dan that there is someone at the main door. "Who do we have here?" he says. Dan looks at the security video monitor, sees the kids, and is puzzled. He answers with his NOT Radio voice, "102.8 FM, how can I help you?" Skyler speaks up, "Hello! Yes! We are here to speak with Dan "The Man" Dravenski." Not wanting to entertain fans while doing his live show, he responds, "Yeah, you can get his autograph at any of the event locations we broadcast from. Have a good night." The audio goes silent, and the kids are disappointed.

Jett sees this and takes control. "Nope! That will not do. Let me try," he says. Jett goes to the touch panel and presses the call button. Dan "The Man" Dravenski is not amused but still answers, "Look, kids, come back tomorrow during the day. Thanks." Jett presses the Talk button and smiles, saying. "Tell him it's the Wind Flyers." There is silence on both ends of the line. After a few seconds, Jett hits the talk button, "Hello?" There is a brief pause, then the door buzzes and unlocks for the kids.

The kids open the front door and head into the dimly lit lobby. They all walk into the front lobby and stand in the middle of the room, not knowing what to do except stare at all the posters, gold records, and autographed images on the walls. Each of the kids stares at the others, looking as if to ask, "What do we do?". Right then, we hear Dan "The Man" Dravenski on the lobby speakers. "You're listening to 102.8 FM Primetime Live with me, Dan "The Man" Dravenski. Stay tuned, as I may have a big surprise for my listeners out there." Dan plays another song and walks out of his studio, down a hall, and shouts. "What do you mean you wouldn't let them in!" We see that Dan is arguing with himself as two different people. He continues shouting, "Do you realize who they are? They are the Wind Flyers! You know what you're fired!" he then speaks in another voice, "But sir..." Dan continues as himself, "No! You're fired! Leave out the back door and save yourself the embarrassment." Dan simulates as if he is throwing someone out the back door. As he closes the door, the kids' heads come around the corner of the hallway. Dan turns and is jerked by surprise,

"Holy Toledo!" Skyler speaks, "Sorry, Sir. Are you Dan "The Man" Dravenski?" Apologetically Dan replies, "I am sorry about the mix-up. You can't find good help anymore. You must be the Wind Flyers." Jett responds, "Yes Sir." Come on back to the studio." The kids' faces light up. This was the first for all of them.

The kids find a place to sit or lean in the small studio. Dan begins speaking, "I have enjoyed following your competitions." Surprised, Zoe says, "Really?" Of course, I work with your dad all the time. I do his radio ads. Plus, you think you were the only ones that fly?" Zoe realizes, her dad made the call to the station about the fundraising, "So my dad called you?" Dan responds, "Right after the decision was made. He and I go way back." "Why have we never seen you?" Zoe says. Dan replies. "I go when you are all in school, where I can be incognito. Plus, most of my jumps are out of planes." "Sweet!" Bodhi says with admiration. With a smile, Dan says, "So let's kick this telethon up a notch, shall we?" "Totally," Logan says. Dan puts on his headphones and instructs the kids to do the same. He pulls the microphone up to his face and turns on his Mr. Radio voice, "That was another hit, right here on 102.8 FM, The White Mountain's Original hit station. Boy, oh boy, do I have a surprise for you? As you know, I started raising money for a group of amazing young kids on tonight's show. Well, they just happen to be here right now. Just so you know where your donations are going, tell us who you are. Logan begins, "I'm Logan Fletcher." "I'm Draven Pierce. Hi Mom!" Draven says. Lilly introduces herself, "Is this really live? Oh yes, I'm Lilly Parker, and this is my brother Jett Parker." Jett replies, "Hi, Everyone, and this is Skyler." With her mesmerizing smile into the microphone she says, "Hi everyone, I'm Skyler Jenkins." And then Zoe, "I'm Zoe McAdams." With a smirk and raised eyebrow Bodhi says, "And I'm Bodhi Thatcher, the good-looking one, and we are." The team, in unison, says, "Team Wind Flyers from Blueridge High School." Dan starts it off, "That's awesome. Well, you have sure shown the mountain you have what it takes to go, pro, and the mountain will be cheering you on for sure. Now, what are you trying to raise tonight?" Skyler leans into the microphone, "Well, we need to raise at least another $6,000. We've already raised half of the total and got some sponsorship, but we're still short of what we need. We even have shirts for sale as well if you want to really show your support."

Dan jumps back on the microphone, "$6k, huh? Well, do you know what? It's doable, with T-shirts to boot, so come on, my fellow Mountain people —let's make this happen, and remember, these kids will be representing America overseas. Think of it as your Patriotic duty." Zoe smiles and says, "That's what I've been saying."

A barrage of calls comes in as the music plays, and the kids jump on the phones, taking calls and donations one after the other. Bodhi looks perplexed about how to use a landline phone, so Skyler helps him out. Donations are also coming in on their Crowdfunding page. We see the clock coming up at 9 pm. The team is scrambling to take calls. Skyler is calculating the donations. Dan is sporting a new Wind Flyers T-shirt for webcams.

Dan gets back on the microphone, "Well, Folks, it looks like a valiant effort. How did we do, team?" Skyler tallies the numbers and says, "$2,132.00, which is amazing, thank you, everyone. On behalf of the team, we are so grateful." Dan jumps in. "That's what we are all about here at 102.8 FM: Helping our local people in any way we can." Dan plays a new track that contradicts the mood of the room. Dan pushes the microphone away, takes off his headphones, and looks at the kids, who seem deflated from the outcome. Dan tries to lift their spirits, "Man, I'm Sorry, guys, we tried. You still have time to raise the rest, though, right?" "Yes, Sir, it's just turning out to be a bit harder to pull this off than we thought," Jett says.

The kids follow Dan out to the lobby, and he does his best to impart some wise DJ wisdom, "Look, I got a few years on you. Actually, I have years on all of you, and what I've learned in life is that no matter what happens to you, it's all about how you react. Are you going to let it get the best of you, or are you going to cowboy up and take it head-on? So, we didn't reach the goal. It was a long shot on short notice." Lilly looks at Dan and says, "And we do appreciate the help." Dan replies, "It's all good. It was my pleasure to help. Not all hope is lost. Everything happens for a reason, they say. Maybe the cosmos wants you to work a little harder for the money, or it's a test of faith to see if you can hold on. I don't know for sure, but I'm about to be off the clock and out the door for a four-day Weekend. (Singing) Everybody's working for the weekend!" The kids look at Dan, not knowing what to say. Dan, flustered, says, "Working for the weekend? Loverboy? No one? I need to have a talk with your parents about proper musical upbringing." The kids thank Dan, and they head out. Dan waves goodbye to them, and they go out the front door. Dan hears the phone lines ringing and goes back to the studio to take one more call before he clocks out.

Dan answers the phone in his radio voice, "102.8 FM Dan, 'The Man' Dravenski, what can I do for you this evening?" An older female voice comes on the phone line, "Yes, is this Mr. Dravenski?" Dan, realizing this woman is old enough to be his mother, goes into a normal Dan voice, "Yes, ma'am, it is. How may I help you this evening? The older female's voice says, "I have been trying to get through to you all night. You must be a well-sought-out man." Dan laughs. "You're too kind, Ma'am. We just have twenty-eight lines. Ten are not fully functional half the time. But we do get calls 24/7. How may I help you?" She continues, "Yes, I wanted to enquire..."

Chapter 9

<u>MYSTERY VISITOR</u>

The kids are in practice. Coach Tanner is running the kids through their routines. An older woman is sitting at a table, drinking a hot beverage, writing in a notepad, and admiring what they can do in the chamber. Music is playing, and the kids get in a good practice. Coach Tanner McAdams notices the older woman.

Coach McAdams addresses the team, "All right, team, bring it in." The team gathers around the coach. Coach continues, "It has been a roller coaster the past two weeks, I know. But all of you have busted your butts on training and raising funds for this competition tour. I know we are still shy, but we still have time. So, on that note, I heard through the Grapevine that there's a lake party tomorrow after school. Instead of Friday night Practice, you all go to the lake together as a team. Just look out for each other and be safe. Deal?" The team agrees. He goes on, "Oh yeah, one more thing. I know we're still short, but I was able to get us some sponsors." Tanner removes a tablecloth that was draped over some boxes. "If we're going to represent our country, then let's do it right." Coach says. The kids are ecstatic and start

1028 Publishing House © 2025

rifling through the boxes, finding their new suits and helmets.

After a few minutes, the kids start heading out the door to go home. The older woman waits patiently at a table in the corner of the room, waiting for her moment to approach Tanner. She walks up to the counter, and Tanner greets her. "Hello, welcome to iFly. I'm the Owner, Tanner McAdams. How can I help you?" The esteemed lady replies, "Why yes, Mr. McAdams, I am rather curious about your establishment and the team known as the Wind Flyers."

Chapter 10

<u>THINGS HAPPENS FOR A REASON</u>

The kids are in first period, waiting in their different classrooms, waiting for the bell to ring. The principal comes on the intercom system with morning announcements. "Good morning, Yellow Jackets. It's turning into a glorious Friday. And whatever you do, don't forget to attend Future Career Day today after School in the gym. It will be out of this world. Many of the kids in different classrooms are not paying attention. Principal Wallace is about to finish the announcements when the students hear him say, "All right, that wraps up this Friday morning announcements. Now, will the following students please report to my office? Fear ensues for each of them as their names are called out individually: "Jett Parker, Skyler Jenkins, Bodhi Thatcher, Draven Pierce, Logan Fletcher, Lilly Parker, and Zoe McAdams."

Outside the Principal's office, the entire team is sitting in a row of chairs against the wall. We see the Principal's Secretary carrying a tray into his office with a steaming teakettle, cups, and cookies. She precariously, but with Grace, holds the tray and opens the door. Then she turns around and closes the door behind her. We hear laughter

1028 Publishing House © 2025

in the office. The kids are so confused. The office door opens, and the secretary comes back out. She looks at the kids and says, "Principal Wallace is ready to see you now," looking at Jett. Jett takes a big gulp, and very timidly, he says, "He wants to see me first?" The secretary responds, "No, He wants to see all of you at once." The team members slowly get up, competing to be the last to go through the door, pushing each other out of the way. They all crowd into a small office. The older woman is in the chair across the desk from Principal Wallace, smiling with a cup of tea.

Principal Wallace looks at the kids and begins speaking, "I would ask you all to sit, but as you see, there are not enough seats. Kids, do any of you know who this kind lady is?" Logan tilts his head, looking at the woman, "You do look familiar."

The woman speaks up, "My name is Roxann Patterson. You might have heard of me as Momma Rox Real Estate." It clicks for Draven, and he says, "You're on the billboards around town." "That's right." She replies. Skyler jumps into the conversation, "Sorry if we are a little confused, Mrs. Patterson, but why were we called to the principal's office?" looking at the principal.

1028 Publishing House © 2025

Mrs. Patterson looks to the principal, "Principal Wallace, if I may?" Principal Wallace replies, "The floor is yours, Mrs. Patterson." Mrs. Patterson begins her story, "My husband Paul was in the army in a special elite parachute team known as the Golden Knights. They are well known as the best of the best. He loved flying planes yet loved jumping out of perfectly good planes even more. He was a hero. Eventually, He taught skydiving. He even taught me and got me hooked. But after so many years, jumping out of planes, well, wasn't so highly advised by doctors at our age. Paul believed everyone should experience the art of flight. He passed away during the pandemic, and I have felt compelled to do something in his memory ever since. Last night, I was at home changing channels on the radio. As I was changing stations, I came across Mr. Dravenski's radio program and was drawn to listen. I found myself cheering you on during your radio telethon and tried to call in numerous times to donate in his name, but never got through, until after the broadcast. That's when Mr. Dravenski finally got my call and filled me in on your campaign." Logan asks, "And that was you at iFly, too, wasn't it?" Mrs. Patterson responds, "Yes, it was. I wanted to see your team in action and learn more about your indoor skydiving facility. Mr.

1028 Publishing House © 2025

McAdams was truly kind and helpful with my questions. What really surprised me was that Mr. McAdams said that even this old bird could still enjoy flight without jumping out of a plane. He is actually giving me lessons next week. I went home last night invigorated for the first time in a long time. So, I prayed about it, and it felt right. So, I decided that Momma Rox Real Estate Would Fulfill the Balance of your goal in my Beloved husband's name."

All of the kids are elated and climb over each other to get the first hug from Mrs. Patterson. Principal Wallace is incredibly happy for the team but must still maintain some order. "Well, as fantastic as this is, and it is pretty fantastic, you all need to get back to class now. Thank Mrs. Patterson." All the kids continue thanking Mrs. Patterson as they file out of the office.

1028 Publishing House © 2025

Chapter 11

FUTURE CAREER DAY

Sitting in his chair, Jett is eyeballing the flyer for Future Career Day and watching the clock. It's always the last few minutes of the day that seem to take forever. The bell rings.

Jett is walking down the hallway as fellow students are doing their best to get out of school as quickly as possible to reach the lake. Bodhi, Logan, and Draven, walk up to Jett. "Are you guys ready for the lake?" He says. Logan adds, "This is going to be an epic weekend." "Yeah, the Cousins Brothers just got the Flyboard, Hoverboard, and Aqua Jett Pack package," Bodhi says. Jett stops in his tracks, smiling, "Jett Pack? I'm so in, but I have to take care of something first, then I will catch up later." Bodhi has a sour look on his face, "What could be better than Jett Parker, Jett Packing at the lake?" he says. Jett replies, "I promise I'll be right behind you." Bodhi, now confused, says, "Seriously?" Whispering to Bodhi, Jett says, "It's Future Career Day. Planetary Defense will be there." Bodhi sees it in Jett's eyes and says, "All right, guys. You go on ahead with the girls. Jett and I will catch up." Logan, looking bummed, says, "Really? Alright. We will see you then."

1028 Publishing House © 2025

Inside the gym, we see booths set up along the walls, with vendors promoting their businesses associated with the Space Industry. SpaceX, Virgin Galactic, Air Force, Planetary Defense, Space Marines, Army Golden Knights, The Navy, Brooks Agnew's Space Mining company, General Dynamics, The Voyager Space Station, Lockheed, Blue Origin & Northrop Grumman. There are booths for Robotics, AI, Science and Medicine, Space Construction, Pilots, and space security. Jett and Bodhi are walking and stopping at each booth, listening intently to each spiel.

Bodhi starts to say, "This is usually the time I would ask you what you have gotten me into Jett Parker." Jett replies, "And?" Bodhi smiles, saying, "I won't lie, Bro, this is some pretty sick Shh..." Instantly, Bodhi catches himself as Principal Wallace appears from nowhere, finishing Bodhi's well-chosen words. "Pretty Sick Stuff indeed, Mr. Thatcher." Bodhi agrees, "Yes, pretty sick stuff, Principal Wallace." Principal Wallace responds, "And just so I'm up to date, Sick means cool now, right?" Bodhi snickers, "Yes, Sir, ever since the 90's." Principal Wallace continues, "I am impressed that you made it today. I mean, with the other choice of the lake and all... Oh yes, don't look surprised. Do you actually think I didn't know what was going on with my students? When I was

your age, we had lake weekends too. Jett responds
honestly. "We're going after this, Sir." Principal
Wallace is proud of the boys showing Maturity
about their futures. He goes on, "Well, I appreciate
you showing up. It shows a lot of maturity that you
are thinking of your future. Bodhi, I think your
mom would be impressed to know you are here.
Grab what info you can and have fun at the lake.
The boys respond, "Thanks, Principal Wallace."

Jett and Bodhi walk onto the next booth,
where Brooks Agnew is describing Space Mining.
The next booth is The Gateway Space Station
Project. John Blincow, the President, is explaining
the Wheel Space Station design and how they will
need a wide range of skilled positions, even in the
hospitality field. The next booth they come to is
the Army Golden Knights. They give a quick spiel
and hand Bodhi a brochure about becoming a
Golden Knight. Bodhi gets excited. The next booth
they come to is SpaceX, which gives a spiel about
rockets, Mars, and Starlink. The next booth is the
Air Force/Space Rangers Booth. The recruiter is
finishing up his spiel as the boys walk up, wide-
eyed, considering the possibility of joining.

Chapter 12

<u>SOME GOOD NEWS</u>

Coach Tanner McAdams is cleaning helmets behind the counter when Skyler, Zoe, Lilly, Draven, and Logan come running excitedly. "What are you guys doing here? I gave you the day off so you could go to the lake." Skyler replies, "Coach, you're not going to believe this. Tell him, Zoe." "Tell me what?" Coach asks. Zoe Proudly informs Coach McAdams the good news, "This morning, we were all called into the principal's office. We thought we were in trouble." Skyler jumps back in the conversation, "Instead, we met this awesome lady, Mrs. Patterson, from Momma Rox Real Estate. And she is covering the rest of the money for the trip!" The girls are screaming with joy. Coach is stunned, "So, hold on. You're saying you raised all the money?" Logan responds, "In Full." Coach has a huge smile and says, "Well, Congratulations... wait, where's Jett and Bodhi? Lilly says, "They're at the Future Career Day event." Surprised, Coach says, "Really?" Zoe says, "We just had to share the good news before we all headed to the lake, Daddy." Coach is ecstatic, "Well, I'm proud of you kids. But you're not out of the woods yet. Now that we have the funds, on

1028 Publishing House © 2025

Monday afternoon, it's back to training. Enjoy yourselves this weekend."

The kids leave for the lake, and Coach Tanner McAdams makes a phone call. The phone is ringing. It's Annie's voicemail, "Hello Sunshine, I just wanted you to know I have big news to share with you, and we're doing it over dinner. I'll be by to pick you up in an hour." We see Tanner go back behind the counter and through a doorway into his office. We hear him rustle through some drawers and then silence. Tanner slowly walks out of his office and out from behind the counter with a box in his hand. He opens it and pulls out a diamond ring. He holds it up to the light to see it sparkle. He smiles, puts it back in the box, then into his pocket. He heads to the Front door, turns out the lights, goes outside, and locks the door.

1028 Publishing House © 2025

Chapter 13

<u>CLASSIFIED</u>

Jett and Bodhi are just finishing up with the Planetary Defense Recruiter, holding a brochure. Jett says, "Thank you, Sir, for all the info. I will talk to my mom about all this." Jett shakes the recruiter's hand, and he and Bodhi both walk away. "So, Planetary Defense, huh? You seemed set on speaking with the recruiter from the start. Isn't there a picture of your dad in the Air Force in your kitchen? I thought you would be a shoe-in. Why don't you talk about your dad?" Jett turns to Bodhi and says with a laugh. "That's Classified." Bodhi is bummed that Jett used his classified line against him. "Ok, man, whatever." "Just don't mention it to anyone. I don't turn eighteen for another month, and I want to talk to my mom first." Jett says. Bodhi replies, "No worries. Your secret is safe with me."

1028 Publishing House © 2025

Chapter 14

AN IMPORTANT DATE

Tanner arrives at the Front door of the Parker house with flowers and rings the bell. We hear high heels walking up to the front door. The door opens, and Annie looks stupendous. Tanner is awestruck. Annie smiles and says, "Well, hello there, Handsome." Blushing Tanner says, "Good evening, my Lady." Annie replies, "Looking pretty dapper, I must say myself. Coach replies, "And you are more stunning than ever." "This charm will get you a long way," she says. With a grin, Tanner replies, "That is the plan. Shall we?" Annie walks out the door, turns, and locks it. The two of them head to the car. Tanner opens the car door for her. She, in turn, leans over to unlock his driver's door. Tanner gets in the car, kisses her, and, with a big smile, says, "Man, do I have something to share with you, but over dinner."

Chapter 15

THE ANNUAL SENIOR DAY

We see the most epic lake party with hundreds of kids from school, Inflatable obstacle courses, zip lines, floats, and party pontoon boats. One of them has a D.J. rocking the party. Wave runners are doing stunts in the water. We see Jett and Bodhi walking down to the beach, taking it all in. Skyler and the girls run up to them, "You made it! I thought you two were going to miss all the fun." "Wait till you do the Obstacle course with the bounce bag. It will launch you so high." Lilly declares. Jett asks, "Where's Draven and Logan?" "Oh, there over there being boys," Zoe says.

Rising out of the lake, Draven and Logan float up on Hydro boards, trying to outdo each other for the girls. Jett is blown away. "Ok, now that's pretty cool. I got to try that. Come on!" Jett says. Jett gestures to everyone to follow him down to the water. Jett reaches the guys in charge of the hydro boards and asks, "Hey, what's up?" The two in charge are twins, Blake and Brent Cousins. Blake replies, "Hey, Bro! Want to give it a go?" "Absolutely!" Jett says. Blake introduces himself and his twin brother, "I'm Blake Cousins, and that's my brother Brent. What's your name?" With a big smile, he replies, "Parker, Jett Parker." Stunned, Blake says, "Wait, seriously, your name is Jett Parker." Blake shouts to his brother Brent on the boat, "Yo, Bro! This kid's name is Jett Parker. No joke! It's time to bust out the big boy." Jett's expression changed to anticipation, "The Big Boy?" Jett says. "Oh yeah!" Blake says, "You are going to love this." Brent Cousins is in the boat and removes a cover to reveal the Hydro Jett pack. Brent pumps up the excitement, "$15,000 of pure adrenaline. With a name like Jett Parker, you have to give it a go." A smile comes across Jett's face like a kid in the candy store, "Yeah, Bro, I think I will."

We see the girls on the beach bathing in the sun, jamming out to the DJ's music on a Pontoon boat while watching Jett suiting up in the harness. Skyler locks eyes with Jett, yelling, "Be careful!" Jett can't hear her and yells, "What?" Again, Skyler yells, "Be careful!" Jett responds, "Right! I love you, too."

Brent begins with the instruction for Jett, "Ok, Bro, it's pretty elementary. If you want to go up, squeeze this lever. Think of it as the gas pedal. If you want to come down, release it slowly." Blake chimes in and says, "If not, you come down faster than the crashed UFO in Roswell." "How do

I steer?" Jett asks. Brent replies, "If you want to go left, lean left. If you want to go right, lean to the right. Forward is forward. Got it? Just find your flow and go with it." "So, just lean?" Jett Asks. Blake responds, "Right. See, you got this. He's got this, right, Brent?" Brent replies, "Oh, for sure, easy Peezy." Jett asks, "And this is safe, right?" Blake, with a mischievous grin, says, "Perfectly... Well, if I were to be honest," Jett replies, "Honest is good." Blake starts spitting out percentages, "I would say 60-65% safe." Fear crosses Jett's face. "Wait, what?" Brent cuts him off, saying, "I would say 40-45%, just to be on the safe side of any argument." Jett, petrified, responds, "40-45%!" Blake starts rushing him, "Let's do this, Bro. Start up the wave runners."

At that moment, water starts rushing out of the jet pack, and Jett starts to rise out of the water. Jett's eyes are as wide as they can be as he does not have full control. "Whoa!" he says. Jett starts to get his balance. The crowd cheers Him on. He starts feeling comfortable zipping around, then gets a little too confident and attempts a spiral, only to lose control. The crowd watches in dismay, knowing they can't do anything except watch. Jett loses control, releases the thrust, and falls like a rock into the lake. The Cousins brothers look at each other, and, in unison, they say, "Just like

Roswell." The Cousins Brothers rush to his rescue. Blake swims up to Jett, "Are you all right, bro?" Jett replies, "Yeah. Did I look cool?" Brent laughs, saying, "Yeah, bro, in a Chaos theory kind of way. But don't worry, I got it all in 4K. Boom!" Jett asks, "Can I go again?" "Maybe later, Bro," Brent replies. Jett doesn't push it, "Ok, Bro, Thanks for the ride." Bodhi gets in the water to help Jett out. "Are you ok?" Bodhi asks. Jett replies, "I feel epic, Bro." Bodhi, surprised at Jett's new lingo, "Bro? You did hit the water hard. Let's chill with the girls." Jett agrees, "I'm good with that." They both walk over to the girls.

Skyler asks Jett, "How are you feeling, Superman?" Jett smiles and responds, "That was killer. You should try it." Smiling, she replies, "Sorry, Love, tanning takes priority today over jetpacks. We have to look good when we get to Europe. Oh, and we stopped by iFly and told Coach about Mrs. Patterson's donation." "Cool! What did he say?" Jett asks. Skyler responds, "He was proud of us and wanted us to enjoy the weekend. He even said he was going to take your mom out for dinner to tell her the news and celebrate." With a satisfied look on his face, Jett says, "This has turned out to be one heck of a weekend."

1028 Publishing House © 2025

Chapter 16

<u>UNEXPECTED EVENING</u>

Annie and Tanner are laughing over wine and empty plates. The restaurant is empty, and employees are cleaning up. The waiter comes with the bill. "I can take care of this when you are ready, Sir." The waiter says. Tanner replies, "Thank you." Annie leans in and says, "I can't believe the kids pulled it off in time." Tanner replies, "They truly are amazing kids." Annie agrees, "They really are. How did we get so lucky?" Tanner replies, "Right?" Tanner is starting to look a little sweaty, and Annie, being a surgeon, is starting to show concern. "Sweetie, are you ok? You look a little pale." She says. Tanner, trying to be tough as nails, tries to ease her worry, "I'm fine. I'm just a little nervous." "Nervous? Why on Earth are you nervous?" Annie asks. Tanner starts to look serious as he begins to speak, "Annie, you and the kids came into Zoe's and my life, and it has been the best two and a half years that we have had in a very long time." Tanner continues to sweat, and Annie notices. "Tanner, drink some water. It can wait." She said. Tanner starts to have trouble with his words, "I, I just wanted to say how much I, I, I love you and the ki..ki..kids, and..." At that moment, Tanner looks pale, dizzy, and collapses to the floor. The wedding ring box rolls out of Tanner's hand onto the floor next to him. Annie is in a panic. "Tanner! Tanner! Help! Someone Call 911! Hold on, Tanner, Paramedics are coming. Stay with me, baby!"

Chapter 17

<u>THE CALL</u>

The party has been a blast. All the students are cuddled up with towels and blankets next to the Bonfire, as a young lady sings and a young man accompanies her on guitar. We see Jett and Skyler cuddled together by the fire. "So, you haven't said anything about what happened at Future Career Day," Skyler says. Jett replies, "It was Awesome. There were a lot of cool jobs." "What caught your eye?" she asks. With confidence, Jett replies, "I think I want to join Planetary Defense." Skyler gives a grin, "Planetary Defense, huh?" "Yeah, I was thinking of becoming a Space Pilot," Jett says. "Space Pilot... has a nice ring to it. I think Space Jockey sounds better, though," she replies. Jett laughs and says, "I would have to agree." After a brief pause as they both stared into the bonfire when Skyler presents an option, "Maybe I should join Planetary Defense, too. Then we could travel through the stars together." Jett responds, "A military couple? Hmm." Skyler asks, "What does your mom think?" "I came straight here. I'll talk to her about it when I get home. I turn eighteen next month, and I will be able to make my own decisions then." He said. "But you're still going to

1028 Publishing House © 2025

talk to her, right?" she asks. Jett responds, "Yeah."
"Well, are you excited about your Birthday?"
Skyler asked. With a curious look, Jett asks,
"Why?" She responds, "It's probably going to be
better than today." "I don't know how that's
possible. Today was pretty epic!" Jett Says. Skyler
just gives a big smile.

Right then, Jett's Phone rings. It's his mom.
Jett answers the phone, "Hey Mom, we're having a
great... whoa, Mom, slow down... What! Where
are you? We'll be there as fast as possible. Jett
hangs up the phone. Skyler looks into Jett's eyes
and sees his panic. "What is it, Jett?" Without
hesitation, Jett takes charge, "Grab our things. We
need to find Zoe and the team." Skyler, very
confused, asks Jett, "What happened?" Sternly,
Jett says, "We've got to go! Come on!"

Jett finds Zoe, who is talking to some
friends by boats on the water's edge. He quickly
runs up to her, stands close, and quietly says to her
in her ear, "Zoe, I need you to be strong about
what I'm about to say." Jett gently whispers in
Zoe's ear, and we see tears roll down Zoe's face.

Chapter 18

BIG CHANGES ARE COMING

The kids run into the Emergency Room together, into the lobby area. Jett goes to the Nurse's Station. "I'm Jett Parker. My mother is Doctor Annie Parker." He said. The nurse replies, "Oh yes, Your Mom told us you were coming. Wait here."

The nurse goes off to retrieve Doctor Parker. The group sits down, with Zoe consulting her. Annie comes out to the lobby in her white doctor coat and greets the kids, "Hey, kids. Zoe, Darling, come here." Crying, Zoe runs to Annie, holding her tight, crying her eyes out. Annie softly speaks to Zoe, "I know, Sweetie. This is hard, I know, but you need to be strong. Your dad is conscious and wants to see you. Can you be strong for your dad?" Zoe Wipes away her tears and says, "Yes ma'am." Jett looks into Zoe's eyes and says, "Hey, you got this, Sis." Zoe is surprised and says, "Sis?" Jett smiles & Annie is proud of Jett for such a small but meaningful gesture of love. Annie puts her arm around Zoe and walks her back to see her father.

As they walk down the hallway, Annie explains to Zoe what happened, "Your Father and I were having a wonderful night out to eat. He told me your good news, and we celebrated. We were there for hours. Then, before we were about to leave, your father was about to say something, and he had a stroke, collapsing on the floor." Zoe starts crying again. Annie tries to comfort her, "Try to be strong, baby. I'm right here with you. He can get through this, but you have to be strong for him." With tears in her eyes, she tries to be strong, "Ok." Zoe wipes her tears again before they goes into the room. Annie stops and looks at Zoe and asks, "You ready?" Zoe nods yes.

Annie and Zoe both go into the room. Tanner is all hooked up to wires and tubes, and his left side is paralyzed, but he hears them walk in and turns his head toward the girls. Tanner attempts to speak, but with difficulty. Zoe runs to him and holds him tight crying out, "Daddy." Tanner plays tuff, "Hey sweetheart. Daddy is going to be fine. I know this nice Doctor who says she can heal me." Tanner looks at Annie and attempts to smile. Annie fights the tears. Tanner continues to speak with some difficulty, "Annie is the best Doctor I know... I need you to be strong baby and have faith." Crying, Zoe answers her father, "I can't lose you, Dad. You're all I have left." "Hey, hey, Princess. I'm not going anywhere. I'm going to be back on the horse in no time. Right, Doc?" Annie wipes the tears away

1028 Publishing House © 2025

responding, "Darn Straight Coach!" Tanner tries to reassure Zoe, "See, baby, it will all work out... I need you to hear me when I say things are going to get a little shaken up, but it's ok. I need you to trust your Daddy, ok?" "What do you mean?" Zoe asks. Tanner responds, "There are going to be some big changes now. You need to have faith and trust your old man." With a stiff upper lip, she says, "Ok, Daddy." "Let the team know I'm going to be ok. I need to talk to Annie now." Tanner says. Zoe leans in, "Love you, Daddy." Tanner smiles and says, "I love you too, Princess." Zoe leaves the room and closes the door.

"She's a very strong young lady," Annie says. Tanner replies, "She gets it from her mother." I need you to do something for me." "Of course, anything," Annie says. Tanner asks, "I need you to call Stan. I need to see him."

Chapter 19

<u>THE FAVOR</u>

It's a beautiful morning in Stockholm, Sweden, at the world's first Wingsuit Training Facility. Stan Ripley is training individuals how to fly wingsuits in the world's only Wingsuit training facility in Stockholm, Sweden. While he is teaching, a fellow employee interrupts him to let him know he has a call. Stan excuses himself, heads down the hall to a reception desk, and takes the call. His head falls into his hands in disbelief.

Stan heads to Stockholm Airport, hoping to catch the next available flight back to the states. He was lucky to catch a flight back to Phoenix, than taking the small puddle-jumper plane from there to Show Low Airport.

The small plane lands at Show Low Airport. We see Stan step off a small 6-seater prop plane. A local Uber picks him up and takes him to Summit Hospital.

Stan comes up to the bedroom door window and looks through the glass at Tanner on the bed, all wired up. He opens the door, walks in, and takes a seat next to his old friend. Tanner wakes up to see Ripley. "You know, pulling a stunt like this just to get me to come home is a little excessive, don't you think?" says Stan. Tanner attempts to roll his eyes. Stan continues, "Well, I'm here. I would ask how you were feeling, but I'm guessing it's a 'not as bad as its looks' kind of situation, right? I'm just saying." Tanner attempts to laugh, and then Stan laughs with him as he leans to hug Tanner. And says, "I have missed you, brother." Stan stands back up. Tanner does his best to speak, but with some difficulty. "Where have you been?" Stand responds, "I jumped around a bit in Europe and wound up teaching at the Stockholm Wind Tunnel. That's where Annie found me." "I'm glad she did," says Tanner. Stan smiles. Tanner continues, "I know you have a life of your own Stan, but as my friend, I need to ask you to do something very important." Stan looks at his friend and declares, "I won't be the Executor of your will." With a dead stare, Tanner says, "Really? My Will? No, Stan. I'm going to be fine. Annie said I can come back from this, and I believe her. The Favor I need you to do for me is even more important." At that moment, Zoe comes into the room with Annie. She is shocked to see Coach Stan Ripley in the room with her dad. "Dad, what's going on?" Tanner continues to speak with some trouble. I asked Annie to contact Stan, and that is why he is here. I wanted to see my old friend.

1028 Publishing House © 2025

Shocked, Zoe responds, "Old friend?" Tanner nods his head. Stan explains, "Your Father and I go way back. Your Mom, too. We were all on a team called." Zoe finishes his sentence, "The Fireflies." "Yes, that's right," Stan confirmed. Bewildered Zoe says, "I never realized it was you in the team photo. You look so different." Stan laughs, "It's called getting old." Tanner starts to laugh in pain, and Zoe runs to hold him tight. "Daddy! Are you ok?" Tanner responds, "Yes, baby. Now watch the hoses." Zoe didn't realize she was squeezing him so tightly, it was messing with the oxygen tubes. "Sorry, Daddy."

Tanner continues speaking, "I'm glad you're all here, so I just have to say this once. Zoe, remember I said there were going to be some big changes?" Zoe replies, "Yes, Daddy." Tanner goes on, "Well, this is one of them. Zoe, I need you to let the team know that Coach Ripley is the new Coach of the Wind Flyers, at least for now. Zoe is taken aback by what her father said, "What?" Stan's eyes grow wide with shock, not expecting this at all. Stan speaks up, "Wait, Tanner, I can't." But Tanner cuts him off. "Stan, please. I wouldn't trust my kids with anyone else. You need to coach them, get them to their competitions overseas, and bring them home safely. I trust you more than anyone. Stan did not expect this at all, but this was his best friend. "I will need to make some calls and ask for some vacation time," Stan said. Tanner looks at his friend and grabs his hand, "Thank you, Stan."

Chapter 20

<u>SURPRISE ENCOUNTER</u>

Skyler and her mother, Rachel Jenkins, are sitting in the waiting room waiting for Zoe. Skyler looks and sees Zoe coming down the hall. Skyler and Rachel stand up. Skyler walks over to Zoe to hug her. Rachel is frozen, staring at the Man walking behind Zoe. Rachel then has a flash from her past.

It's 2004, at a drop zone in Belgium. We see a noticeably young Rachel Jenkins with purple hair and an incredibly young Stan Ripley with thick hair. They have just done a jump with eight other people from around the world. Their adrenaline is pumping, and they are all in good spirits as they pull their chutes off the ground. The two of them catch each other's eyes and smile.

Later that night, the flyers are in lawn chairs around a campfire, drinking and caring on. We see Rachel sitting with some other female flyers. There is an empty chair next to Rachel. Music is playing in the background, and we see the young Ripley come over to her. "Is this seat taken?" he asks. Rachel replies, "No, go ahead." Stan is surprised and asks, "American?" "Yes." She replies. "I'm Ripley," he says. Rachel responds, flirting, "They call me Angel." "They?" he asks, "Yeah, the powers that be? Don't question it; just accept it." Rachel smiles flirtatiously. Stan concedes, "I can do that. By the way, I love your purple hair, Angel." She responds, "Thanks." Rachel and Stan continue their conversation as the music slowly drowns them out.

It's early morning, and the sun is shining through a hotel room window. The Sun is shining on Rachel's face as she lays peacefully in bed. She slowly opens her eyes, holding her head in her hand. Rachel is experiencing a nasty hangover. Without moving her head, she scans the room with one eye and notices that this is not her room. She tries to move and realizes she is not alone. She looks over her shoulder and sees Stan lying quietly on the bed next to her. She slowly maneuvers her way out of bed and quietly gathers her things and heads out the front door.

Back in the lobby, Rachel comes out of her flashback and sees Ripley standing in front of her with Zoe and Skyler, who look confused. "Hi, I'm Stan Ripley. I'm an old friend of Tanner's." Rachel responds, "Hi... I'm Skyler's Mom, Rachel, Rachel Jenkins." The two shake hands. Rachel is internally petrified. Stan smiles, and his head tilts, analyzing Rachel's face and asks, "I'm sorry, have

we met before? I feel like I have seen you before."
Rachel is really freaking out now, but doing her
best not to show it, while Skyler notices something
different with her mother. Skyler chimes in and
says, "Most likely at the competitions." Rachel
liked the answer and ran with it, "Right!, The
competitions." Skyler continues the conversation:
"Coach Ripley used to coach Precision Flight."
Stan speaks up, "I used to, unfortunately, I had a
team that became toxic, and I moved on. I teach
Wingsuit classes in Stockholm now. Surprised,
Rachel responds, "Stockholm, Sweden?" "That's
correct." Says Stan.

Rachel takes a chance and tries to get
answers from Stan: "Do you have family, Mr.
Ripley?" Stan smiles and says, "You can just call
me Ripley." Rachel replies, "Ok, Ripley. Do you
have a wife or a family?" He replies, "I've had an
amazing life, but I was never blessed with love and
Family. My family has been the Flyers of the
world that I train and fly with." Rachel's internal
freak-out session starts to subside. Then Stan asks
in return, "How about you? Is there a Mr.
Jenkins?" "No, Mr. Jenkins, as you put it, was
never in the picture." She said. "Ah! Well, it was
nice to meet you, Ms. Jenkins." Stan said with a
smile. Rachel responds, "You can call me Rachel."
Stan replied, "I will do just that. Rachel, it was

nice to meet you. Skyler, Zoe, I will see you tomorrow." Stan walks away as Rachel watches, and Skyler asks Zoe, "What did he mean by I'll see you tomorrow ?" Zoe responds, "We need to talk."

1028 Publishing House © 2025

Chapter 21

<u>A SHOCK TO THE SYSTEM</u>

The kids slowly enter the practice area, where Zoe and Rachel are waiting. Bodhi asks, "How's coach doing?" Jett chimes in, "Yeah, what's the news?" Showing stress in her face because of what she was about to say, Zoe gathers the strength and starts to inform the team of new changes, "Dad was having dinner with Annie while we were at the lake. Dad started to get pale and then had a stroke. He can talk, but with some difficulty. Annie said the left side of his body is paralyzed." Upset, Jett asks, "Forever?" Zoe responds, "Hopefully not. Your Mom said that with Physical rehab and therapy, he could recover somewhat. But it's going to take him a long time to recuperate. So, I brought you all here to let you know, on my dad's authority, that we will still be going to Europe to compete. But there will be some changes that we will all have to accept." Logan asks the obvious question on everyone's mind: "So, if we're still going to Europe, who is going to be our Coach?" Zoe takes a deep breath and States, "My Father would never trust anyone else to coach us except for one man, who I came to find, surprisingly, is his best friend. An honest and fair man, something we all got to witness personally. He would be the best choice to train us and lead us to victory." The team is completely perplexed, trying to think who it could be. "So, is it someone we know?" Draven asks. Zoe replies, "Yes."

At that moment, Coach Stan Ripley walks into the room. The team's eyes widen in surprise. Bodhi begins to freak out. "No! No! Do you know who he is? His team members broke my arm, remember? Because I sure do!" Logan is stunned and asks, "This is a joke, right? A bad joke?" Stan speaks up, "I'm afraid it's not. Look, I know this leaves a bad taste in your mouth, I get it. But once I learned of my former team's behavior from Coach McAdams, I put a stop to it and walked away. Never to train with them again. But you guys have heart and determination, and I respect that. Annie and Tanner told me about how you have raised the money for this trip. I've been to Europe and can show you the ropes. If you still want to go." They all look at each other, then Jett speaks up, "He did disqualify his team at the championship, remember?" Stan speaks again, "That should show you that I will not put up with that crap! But you are the Wind Flyers, and I don't expect that from you, or should I?" The team all says, "No, Sir." Jett comments, "We like to think we are better than that."

1028 Publishing House © 2025

Stan replies, Excellent, that was what I wanted to hear. Then we understand each other? I shouldn't have to worry about ill will, right?" The team once again says, "No, Sir." Stan says, "I think we are going to do just fine."

The kids continue staring at one another skeptically. Then Skyler speaks, "I say we give him a chance, for Coach." The team agrees. Jett asks, "All right, Coach, what's next?" Stan shows a sigh of relief and says, "Well, as Coach McAdams would say, practice, practice, practice. Plus, I need to find out what I'm working with. I will see you all here tomorrow at 6 O'clock."

Chapter 22

<u>SHOW ME WHAT YOU CAN DO</u>

Coach Ripley meets with the team in the practice room. "All right, is everyone here?" Coach asks. Zoe replies, "All here, Coach." Stan begins his speech, "First, I just want to say thank you for showing up. Second, I checked in on Coach McAdams; he is doing better and is glad we are all working together moving forward. Now let's see what you got."

A song starts to kick everything into high gear, and the team starts showing Coach Ripley of what they are capable.

Coach Ripley grabs a notepad and pen and sits outside the chamber. The kids are playing rock, paper-scissors to see who goes first. Coach Ripley gestures for them to hurry up. Logan goes first even though his nerves are shot from stress. Logan Panics and double-checks his shoes to make sure his laces are tied this time. He closes his eyes, takes a deep breath, and his heart rate slows down. He jumps in. The team is cheering him on as they shake their fists in the air to the beat. Other onlookers are headbanging to the bass. Logan releases all his stress and decides to just have some fun. Logan gets into the groove of the music and the crowd's energy, delivering a worthy performance. He exits the chamber with a smile on his face. In the holding room, the others cheer him on as he enters. Logan stops and turns to the team to say, "Don't go in there just for points. Have fun. It's so much easier." The team smiles at each other.

Lilly shouts out, "Who's next?" Zoe speaks up, "I'll go next." Zoe proceeds to the chamber door opening while adjusting her head cover under her helmet. She waits till the controller gives her the thumbs up. The fan revs up, and her music track begins. Zoe comes into the chamber hard, like a gangster, to a hip-hop beat. The team is doing a dance that all the kids today do to this song.

Coach Ripley notices the team's camaraderie and likes it. Three-quarters of the way through Zoe's hip-hop routine, Skyler comes in, and the two do a well-choreographed Segway between the two flyers and two different songs. At the end of Zoe's song, Zoe exits the chamber, leaving Skyler by herself with no music. Skyler is slowly spinning while lying on her side in a sleeping position. The music starts, and Skyler does an air ballet that entertains everyone watching. Coach Ripley is impressed. She exits the Chamber. Everyone starts clapping and cheering. Coach Ripley looks at Skyler and gives her a nod of approval. Skyler nods in her helmet.

Next is Bodhi and Draven doing a 2-way performance to an N.F. style rap song, and it's off the hook. Lots of slapstick while having a Breakdance competition in the Air Chamber, which was much better than the 2024 Olympics. Lilly jumps into the chamber, acting as a judge who is flying around them as they have an Air Dance-off. The audience is really getting into the performances. The three of them fly out the Chamber door like pros right as the song ends.

There is silence, and Jett is now the last to go. Jett hears Logan's voice in his head. "Just have fun". The Controller gives the thumbs up. Jett cues for his music. A song Jett used to listen to while doing Parkour. The Music comes on with violins and a bass line. Jett puts his helmet on and walks to the chamber entrance, falling into the chamber sideways, and stops just hovering above the net. He walked in circles along the glass wall, his head tilted as if he were thinking. Then the beat kicks in a hard Dubstep Beat, and Jett busts out in dance, flying, and doing Parkour to a sick beat with EDM Horns and bass. He is tearing it up. Everyone in the building, seeing this, knew they were witnessing something special. Stan is blown away and can only say, "Holy Moley." He tries not to seem impressed, but Skyler catches him amazed by Jett's new style. The song ends, and Jett exits the Chamber. All the kids come over to Coach Ripley to hear what he thinks.

Lilly speaks first, "So?" Coach Ripley responds, "So, what?" Lilly stares at Ripley and says, "You know, you can say it." Ripley plays dumb, "Say what?" Lilly Smiles victoriously, "That was pretty awesome." Coach Ripley replies, "Well, it wasn't bad." Lilly gives him the stare that only women know. Coach Ripley finally caves, "Yes, Lilly, I will say it was awesome." The team smiles and laughs. Coach Ripley continues, "Look, you guys are good, I'll give you that, and that just means," The team looks jovial while Coach Ripley continues, "This will not be as hard as I thought. Jett, what did you do in there? I have never seen anything like that." Jett replies, "It's something Coach McAdams and I would work on late at night. It was Top Secret, but since you're now our coach, I figured you might as well see it."

Coach Ripley is at a loss for words, "Well, I'll be, Coach McAdams really did have a special Ace up his sleeve. Well, this is good to know. So, what was that again, Jett?" Jett answers, "Parkour, it's Free Running. It's what I used to do before I moved here." At this point, the wheels in Coach Ripley's head are turning while he asks, "So you were one of those guys running along ledges and jumping from building to building?" "Yes Sir." Jett responds. Coach Ripley says, "Parkour in the Chamber. Brilliant." Jett Smiles. Coach Ripley looks around at his new team, seeing in his mind all the talent and potential in front of him. He smiles and says, "I would be lying if I said I wasn't impressed. So, tonight was, let's call it, an audition, and you all passed. Anyone hungry?

1028 Publishing House © 2025

Chapter 23

<u>A GLITCH IN THE MATRIX</u>

The Team is sitting at a large table made up of many little tables brought together. Two Pizza servers deliver four large, fully loaded pizzas to the table and say, "Here you go guys. Four, steaming hot, fully loaded supreme pizzas." "Oh yeah!" Jett says. The kids dig in like savages. Strings of cheese from the pizza slices are stretched across the table. The two Pizza servers look at the table like they just dropped a cow into a velociraptor cage.

Coach Ripley tries to gain control, "Guys, Guys! Ladies, you too. There's enough for everyone. Skyler?" Skyler looks up from the feast with a mouthful of pizza, replying to the coach, "Yes, Coach." Coach Ripley says to her, "Whatever our Food budget is for the trip, double it. Can you pass me a slice, please?"

Skyler grabs a slice of pizza for herself and Coach. Both of them take their pizza and put it on their plates. Then, both of them are in unison, without even noticing the other, as they both grab one of the many Parmesan canisters on the table near them. Then, both of them drenched their pizza in Parmesan and Ranch dressing. Bodhi noticed this and looked puzzled. Then Coach and Skyler both tear the crusts off their pizzas, roll them up, and eat them like burritos. Bodhi starts to laugh. Jett asks him, "What's so funny?" Laughing, Bodhi responds, "Just saw a glitch in the Matrix." Jett, missing what was happening, just says, "Ok, man."

The kids and their new coach have a great time laughing and singing to the music playing in the restaurant. Jett looks over to Coach Ripley, who is smiling and having a good time. Ripley looks at Jett and gives the Nod.

1028 Publishing House © 2025

Chapter 24

A BIRTHDAY SURPRISE

The team is training, working hard in their classes, and planning their route in Europe. Annie and Tanner are receiving physical therapy at the hospital. Tanner is slowly progressing. The team is practicing and has brief moments where Skyler and Coach do the same things or display the same mannerisms at the same time. By the third time, some of the team, including Rachel, who came to pick up Skyler, also noticed the similarities and felt uneasiness. Teammates are starting to notice something off.

It is now 3 weeks later. Skyler and Jett are in her car listening to the radio before the first bell. She turns the radio down and asks Jett, "So, are you Excited about your Big 18 today, Man of mine?" Jett laughs at the inside joke, responding, "Yes, and I'm stoked. It's a Friday and a senior half-day. What should we do?" Skyler replies, "You just let me worry about that." Jett is smitten with love, "Have I told you how awesome you are?" Skyler smiles and says, "Not today." Jett kisses her and says, "Well, you're pretty awesome."

Jett goes in for a kiss, and Skyler pauses him, saying, "You're not so bad yourself, Mr. Parker." They kiss, and the first warning bell rings. They get out of her car, and she says, "Meet me here at lunch." Jett agrees, "Sounds like a plan. Love you!" She replies, "Love you too, Birthday Boy."

Chapter 25

MYSTERY CALLER

Annie Parker is in the living room on the phone.
"He has done really well with his grades... I
appreciate you doing this for him... I know it will
be a big responsibility, but he has grown up a lot
since we moved here. He's ready... How's Tanner?
Oh, wow, thank you for asking; that really means a
lot... he is doing better. It is truly kind of you to
ask... But everyone will be there by 4:30 today.
They have a senior half day... Thank you so much.
This is really a big deal. Just know I appreciate it. I
know it's hard with the job... But I got a cake in the
oven and need to get back to it. Good talking to
you... Bye."

Annie hangs up the phone. She goes
upstairs, grabs the linen basket, and proceeds from
room to room, collecting laundry. While getting
clothes in Jett's room, she comes across the
Planetary Defense recruitment brochure. She looks
through it and looks surprised.

Chapter 26

<u>A BIRTHDAY TO REMEMBER</u>

Jett is in the last class before lunch, and the teacher embarrasses Jett by having the class sing Happy Birthday to him. Jett Blushes as the bell rings. Jett is now 18 years old and officially an adult. Jett grabs his things and heads to the Parking lot. On the way, fellow students congratulate him with birthday wishes as he walks by. He replies to the crowd, "Thanks, everyone."

Jett makes his way out to the parking lot, where Skyler is waiting for him. Bodhi's car pulls up next to Skyler's, with everyone crammed in. "Let's get it done. Follow me." He says. Jett is perplexed and asks, "Where are we going?" as he jumps into Skyler's vehicle. Skyler replies, "Babe, you don't worry about a thing. Today, we got you. Just enjoy the day. But there is one catch. Jett looks surprised, "I knew it. What is it?" Jett asks. Skyler smiles, pulls out a blindfold, and says, "When the time comes, you've got to put this on till I tell you to take it off." Jett responds, "Now?" Skyler laughs and says, "No, not yet. When we get down to the valley." "The Valley?" he replied. Skyler continues, "Yep, so we got 3 hours to kill." "So, what are we going to do till we get to wherever we're going?" Jett asks. Skyler has a big grin and says, "Babe, you are going to play some killer tunes while I drive, and we are going to soak up some amazing scenery. When we get close, I will tell you to put on the blindfold."

Skyler smirks at Jett. Jett smiles and pushes play. Another killer track is playing, and the caravan drives on down the mountain.

Driving down the beautiful route from the mountains to the desert, the kids are singing along to the music. Once they reach the valley and reach the main highways. The Traffic is thick. A big difference that the kids were not used to on the mountain. Jett speaks up, "Man, I forgot how crazy the city and traffic were. Flatlanders, as far as I can see."

Skyler looks at Jett and hands him the blindfold. "Jett, it's time," she says. "For what?" Jett replied. "The blindfold," she said. Jett responds, "Oh yeah, right?" Not fully sure, Jett puts on the blindfold. Skyler tries to ease his concerns, "We will be there soon."

It is a hot day in the valley. We see the kids' vehicles pull into a local airport, passing the sign at the Entrance that reads "Phoenix Air Show." The kids park in a packed parking lot. We hear a stunt plane buzz the audience. It is Kirby Chambliss.

1028 Publishing House © 2025

The World's best Stunt Pilot for Red Bull is doing his thing to amaze the crowd. Jett is guided by Skyler and the Team through the Entrance and onto the Airport tarmac.

Skyler removes the Blindfold, and Jett's eyes grow wide. He sees Planes of all sorts on the Runway and Promotional Booths to his right. Skydivers are coming in for a landing. Jett is blown away that his friends took him to an air show.

Jett hears the roar of multiple engines. He turns and sees a man in a helmet standing on the runway next to four other men in jet packs. The Show announcer comes on the loudspeaker. "All right, folks, many of you have been waiting all day for this. The newest jet-fueled aviation and Body flight sports. Ladies and gentlemen, I give you Jet Pack Racing!" The crowd goes wild. The announcer continues, "Who do you think will win this race today?"

The crowd starts to cheer, and the horn goes off. All four pilots rise off the ground. With a small Jet engine on each arm and leg, the Jetpack Pilots keep up with each other. The crowd's cheers get louder. Jett is blown away at what he is witnessing. The Jetpack pilots are holding their own, but one wins the race. The pilot does a quick spin in a circle before he lands with a roar of his two mini jet engines on his arms. He lands on his platform and shuts down the engines. Jett goes over to the pilot, who is taking his helmet off, and sees Jett and says, "Pretty cool, huh?" Jett asks, "How long can you fly?" The pilot responds, "Up to 10 minutes." Jett's eyes widen, and he says gleefully, "Wow! So, how could I learn to do this?" The pilot responds, "Well, actually, we have a school in California. You can learn how to do this in a controlled environment." Jett is so impressed, "Really? That's fricken amazing!" Jett said. The pilot continues, "You can grab our brochure and contact info at our booth over there."

Like a kid in a toy store, Jett replies, "Awesome, Thanks." Jett heads over to the booth and grabs the brochures. Skyler catches up to Jett and says, "I don't think I have ever seen such passion in someone to want to fly as bad as you." Jett laughs.

We see Coach Ripley walk up to the kids and says, "Hey, guys! Glad you made it. Happy Birthday, Jett." "Thanks, Coach," Jett replied. Coach continues, "Well, I wanted you to see some real flyers in their element."

Bodhi Points up to the Sky. A Red Bull Stunt plane comes zooming down the runway and shoots straight up into the air, spinning as it climbs higher and higher, doing aerial acrobats, and Bodhi says, "Jett, that's what I want to do when I grow up." With a confused look, Jett says, "Really? I thought you wanted to be a Golden Knight." Bodhi replies, "Who says I can't do both?" Jett agrees, "Yeah, why not?"

Over the loudspeakers, we hear the announcer, "Folks, if you look way up in the sky to your left, you will see a C-130. Keep your eyes on it." Just then, several black dots fall from the Plane. We see the Army's famous elite parachute team, The Golden Knights, drop from a C-130. We watch in amazement as the Golden Knights pull off some serious maneuvers. They pull their chutes and continue to show their amazing skills. The Knights come together and stack themselves on top of each other with smoke flowing from their ankles.

The kids, especially Bodhi, are impressed. They are getting the itch to leave the chamber and jump out of a plane themselves. The Golden Knights land on their marks and start walking back to the booths, carrying their packs and chutes. Stan jogs over to the Golden Knights. The kids watch from a distance. One of the Knights sees Stan, drops his bag, and gives Stan a sturdy shake and a

1028 Publishing House © 2025

hug. They talk for a few seconds, and then Stan waves the kids over.

The team walks over to Coach Stan, who then makes introductions. "This is my old friend that I used to jump with back in the day." Sargent Major Valencia chimes in, "Way back in the day." "This is Sargent Major Valencia," Ripley says. Sargent Major Valencia asks, "Are you guys enjoying the Air Show?" "Totally," Jett says. "It's actually Jett's 18th Birthday today," Ripley says. "Is it now? Well, you're now old enough to Skydive. Have you ever wanted to jump out of a plane?" Sargent Major Velencia asks. Ripley adds, "Jett is actually the Captain of our Indoor Skydiving team." "You don't say. Well, Jett, maybe we will have to jump together sometime." Jett is feeling bliss and says, "Can my friend Bodhi come? He is eighteen, too?" Sargent Major Valencia says, "I think that could be arranged." Bodhi leans into Jett and whispers, "Thanks, Brother." The team says their goodbyes to Sergeant Major Valencia and continues checking out the air show.

"Let's go over by the planes," Skyler suggested. Jett agrees, "ok." The rest of the team catches up to Jett and Skyler on a plane. Skyler is looking around the crowd as if she's searching for someone.

Logan asks Jett, "So Jett, what do you think of your surprise?" Jett replies, "I have always loved air shows." Out of the crowd, standing behind Jett, is a 4-star Air Force General in full uniform. He interrupts Jett, "And I sure loved taking you to them." He said. Jett can't believe his ears and turns around in shock, "Dad!" he hugs him tight, and General Parker says, "Hey son, how are you? Happy Birthday!" Lilly freaks out. "Daddy, you're here!" Lilly joins Jett in hugging their father. Jett says, "We've missed you, Dad." Lilly grabs him tight, "Daddy, you're really here." Holding his children, General Parker says, "I missed you both, too."

The Team is surprised by this as well. Logan speaks up first, "So, you're Mr. Parker?" General Parker responds, "And you all must be the Wind Flyers. I have heard a lot about you. I'm Jett and Lilly's father, General Parker. It's a pleasure to finally meet you all. It would have been sooner, but my job keeps me on the move constantly." Intrigued, Bodhi asks him, "So what do you do as a 4 Star General?" General Parker gives a small grin and says, "I would so love to tell you...But it's

Classified." Bodhi turns to Jett and says, "So you weren't kidding." Jett smiles and says, "I told you."

Hello, Sir, my name is Stan Ripley. General Parker reaches out to shake his hand, replying, "Ah, yes, their new Coach. It's nice to meet you. So, you're the one who took over after Tanner's Stroke?" "Yes, Tanner and I go way back. After the stroke, he asked me to take over the team until he recovered." Stan said. "Look, here is my card with my cell. While you're in Europe, if you need anything, let me know." General Parker said, "Thank you, Sir. I will be sure to do that. Will you be in the area?" Stan responds. "I never know where I'll be next. So, we will see." General Parker said.

Lilly looks up to her father and asks, "How long will you be here, Daddy?" General Parker looks down at his baby girl and says, "Well, sweetie, just for an hour or two. Then I have to catch a plane to Colorado Springs. "So, what are you doing here in Phoenix?" Jett asks. His father replies, "I have a meeting in 20 minutes that I have to attend, then back to Cheyanne Mountain. But while I was in town. I needed to pick something up. Want to see it?" excited Jett says, "Sure."

The kids follow the General as he walks over to the parking lot. General Parker continues,

"Your mom says you have shown so much improvement since you moved to the mountain." "Well, it's a different world compared to Dallas. The people are different. Things go more slowly, and the people are kinder. Mom swears it's altitude. Plus, Skyler is in my life now, and that makes it all worthwhile." Jett replies. "Yes, Skyler. So, is it serious between you two?" his father asked. Lilly chimes in and says, "Pretty serious." "Really?" her father asked. Lilly continues, "They will probably get married." Shocked, her father says, "You don't say." Jett butts in, "Lilly!" Lilly replies, "Everyone knows you two will end up together."

General Parker changes the subject, "How's school for you, Lilly?" Lilly responds, "Sometimes, I wish I could just skip grades." General Parker hugs her tight and says, "My little Brainiac. I'm so proud of you, too!"

The kids and the General come to a stop in the parking lot as all their eyes gaze on the beauty of a new 2023 BMW 760i X-Drive in pure metallic gray, with all the bells and whistles. The kids swarm around the car, completely impressed.

Like Bob Barker, the General begins to go over the vehicle's impressive specs. "This is the 2023 BMW 760i X-Drive. 21-inch M

1028 Publishing House © 2025

Aerodynamic Jet Black Style 909 Wheels, Luxury Rear Seating Package, Driver Assistance, Executive package, automatic doors, Bowers & Wilkins Diamond Surround Sound System, and Massage seats." "Holy Crap, this is more expensive than my house," Bodhi says. General Parker looks at the kids and says, "Work hard, and you can drive something like this." Jett encourages his father's hard work, "You have worked hard for a lot of years, Dad," he said. General Parker responds with, "Yes, that's true, But You have worked hard, too, Jett, your mother and I appreciate your hard work and determination. So, on that note, it's your 18th Birthday today, and you are officially an adult now. I think it is time that you have an adult gift." General Parker hands the BMW keys to Jett. Jett doesn't know what to say. The rest of the kids are spazzing out. 'No way!" Logan shouts. Bodhi's eyes sparkle looking at the BMW and says, "Oh, yes! I call Shotgun. General Parker, please adopt me!" "I can't wait to step out of this bad boy at school. The kids are going to freak out!" Lilly says.

Jett is in utter shock and asks, "Dad, seriously?" General Parker smiles proudly and says, "You are turning into the man we hoped for. Thank you." Jett replies, "Thank you, Dad." General Parker replies, "Thank your mom and

Skyler, they help set this up." Skyler smiles, hugs Jett, and gives him a kiss. Skyler says, "I told you it would be a great day. Happy Birthday." Jett is on cloud nine, "Thank you," he says. Skyler kisses him on the cheek and says, "Anything for you, babe."

General Parker speaks up, "I know this was sudden and brief, but I do have to get to my meeting. But I will see you again soon. I love you both." General Parker hugs his kid's goodbye and heads off into the crowd.

Lilly asks, "This is awesome. Can I ride with you back up the mountain?" Jett agrees, "Sure, Lilly. Skyler, will you be my co-pilot?" Skyler smiles and says, "Always... Zoe! Drive my car back, please." Bodhi is bummed, "But I called Shotgun." Jett puts his hand on Bodhi's shoulder and says, "Sorry, Bodhi. My lady gets first dibs to sit shotgun on the first ride." Bodhi pouts a little and says, "Fine."

As the group disperses, we see Coach Ripley left alone, and saying to himself, "Yeah, I'll be fine. Don't worry about me. You kids have fun. I'm just going to go over here."

Bodhi shouts from the car, "Later, Coach!" Coach replies, "Ah, later, I guess." Bodhi and Lilly get in the back. Draven is driving Skyler's car with Zoe,

1028 Publishing House © 2025

and Logan is driving Bodhi's car. The Sun starts to set on the mountain tops as the team drives the three cars back up to the mountain. Music is blaring, and the kids are all in good spirits.

Chapter 27

<u>A MOTHER'S WORRY</u>

Jett pulls up to his driveway in his new car. Logan pulls up to the street curb in Bodhi's car. Bodhi gets out of Jett's new car along with Skyler with Lilly. Zoe pulls up behind them in Skyler's car. Jett takes a moment after turning off the ignition to soak up what a great day it was, and that this was really his car. "Happy Birthday, Jett. I'll see you later." Bodhi says, while opening the driver's door, "Scoot over, Logan." Bodhi gets in. Draven leans over and says, "Happy Birthday, Jett. By Lilly." Jett replies, "Thanks, man." Lilly looks into Draven's eyes, saying, "Bye, Draven." The boys drive off as Zoe is next in line in Skyler's Car, waiting on Skyler. "Are you coming, Skyler, or do I just keep the car?" Zoe asks. Skyler replies, "Hold on, I'm coming."

Skyler gets close to Jett, "Happy Birthday, Baby." Skyler plants a kiss on Jett, then turns and walks away. She gets in her car with Zoe and drives off.

Annie is sitting in her kitchen waiting for the kids. She starts to light the candles on Jett's Birthday cake. The kids come in through the front door, and Annie starts singing. "Happy Birthday to You, Happy Birthday to You. Happy Birthday, dear Jett. Happy Birthday to you." Jett has a big smile on his face. Annie says, "Blow out the candles, Jett." Jett blows out the candles. Annie continues to instruct Jett, "Now grab a plate and fork, and let's dig into this cake."

At the Jenkins residence, we see Rachel with a box full of pictures from her earlier life as a skydiver, spread across the kitchen table. With a Martini by her side, she sits at the table with tears in her eyes while she stares at a picture of a Skydiving team in Belgium in 2004. We see the Young Stan Ripley and, on the other side of the picture, a young Rachel Jenkins, A.K.A. Angel. She wipes away the tears as Skyler walks in the front door. "Hey, Mom." Rachel wipes the rest of the tears from her face before she responds. 'Hey Baby. How was the Air Show? Was Jett Surprised?' Skyler smiles big and continues, "He was blown away, Mom. But the big surprise was his dad showed up in uniform and gave him a new BMW." Rachel's Jaw drops, and she says, "Wow!" Skyler goes on, "Well, his dad is a four-star general in the Air Force, and the pay is pretty decent." Rachel agrees, "I would say so."

Rachel gets closer to her mom and says, "Mom, are you crying? What are you doing?" With tears in her eyes, Rachel replies, "Oh, sweetie, I'm fine. I was just going through this box of memories with the help of 2 Margaritas, and the waterworks started. Skyler goes over and hugs her mom. "It's Ok, Mom, I'm here." Rachel looks into Skyler's eyes and asks, "Do you resent me for the fact that you never had a dad in your life?" No, mom, why would you ask that?" Rachel holds her hands and continues, "I would just never want you to hate me for it." Skyler now looks into her mother's eyes and says, "Mom, look, you have done a great job. Have you not heard I'm a Bad Ass?" Rachel laughs and says, "Yes, baby, I do know." Skyler continues to uplift her mother, "You did the best a single mother could do. Any father figure in my life was Coach Tanner, and to be honest, our new coach, Coach Ripley, turned out to be a really good guy and a great coach. I can't explain it, but we just seem to click. Like we're on the same wavelength. Does that make sense, or is that weird?"

Rachel's eyes swell with an ache inside her, and she says, "No, baby, that's not weird at all. I'm

1028 Publishing House © 2025

glad your new coach is working out." Rachel looks down at the picture and then swiftly puts it with all the pictures back in the box as she continues speaking, "Well, baby, do you know what? The one thing that I know is true and forever?" What's that, Momma?" Skyler replies. Rachel smiles big and says, "I will always love you." Skyler hugs her and says, "I love you too, Momma. They hug each other tight. Wiping away the tears, Rachel asks, "Are you excited about Europe?" Yes ma'am." Skyler replies. Her mother continues, "That's my baby girl. You're going to do great; I just know it."

Down the street, Jett is helping his mother with the dishes. Annie asks, "So, was it the best birthday ever?" Jett grins big and says, "Yeah, it was." "Did you enjoy seeing your dad?" she asked. "Yeah, even though it was brief." He said. His mother goes on, "And what about the Car? Did we do ok?" Jett's grin turns into a big smile and says, "Better than ok!" Annie puts the dishes away, then says, "Well, you have earned it.

Annie sits at the table and gestures for Jett to sit down, too. She begins. "Jett, can we talk about something now that you are a legal adult?" Just replies, "Sure." Annie continues, "I was grabbing your laundry, and I came across this on your desk." Annie puts the Planetary Defense

Recruitment Brochure on the counter. Jett responds, "Yeah, I was actually going to talk to you about it when I got back from the lake, but coach had his stroke, and it fell on the back burner.

Annie says, "That's understandable. So, let's talk about it now." Jett stammers a little and begins speaking, "Ok... I really want to be a part of the Planetary Defense Force and be a space pilot." Annie's eyes grow wide, and she says, "A space pilot! You are definitely your father's son. Look, do you really love Skyler?" "You know I do," he says. Annie asks the next question, "Do you plan to marry her?" "Sure, one day?" Jett replies. Annie starts getting serious, "Do you think that Space Force will have Family Housing in space? Honey, you're an adult now, making adult decisions that require you to think through things. I won't be there to hold your hand. You will be making the calls from now on. But if you genuinely love Skyler, keep her in mind and think about the stress on your relationship. I'm just saying. I'm speaking from experience as a former military wife. Just put some thought into it before you make any life changing decisions.

1028 Publishing House © 2025

Chapter 28

<u>EUROPE, HERE WE COME</u>

All the kids and their parents, along with Coach Ripley, are in the baggage claim area by the TSA security entrance. Tanner is in a wheelchair with Annie pushing. Coach Ripley addresses the team, "Ok, before we say our goodbyes, let's do a quick checklist. Does everyone have their passports, visas, and Plane tickets?" Everyone holds up their Tickets and passports. Coach Ripley continues, "Check. Now, does everyone have their luggage and gear bags?" Everyone holds up their gear bag and luggage. Coach Ripley continues, "Check. Travel money? Don't show me the money, just give me a thumbs up." Everyone puts their thumbs up. Coach Ripley goes on, "And lastly, do you all have your plug converters? The electric plugs are different from ours." Half the team realizes they don't have adapters. Coach Ripley shakes his head, "Ok, we still have time. Suppose you don't have a converter and need one. Buy one quickly at that store over there and come right back to this spot. We have 20 minutes before we need to get in that insane line" pointing to TSA. "Anyone else who needs to use the restroom, go now, and we will all meet back here."

Everyone disperses, and the parents stay behind with their luggage. Rachel goes over to Stan. And asks, "Stan, can I talk to you over here for a moment?" Stan obliged her, "Sure." Rachel takes Stan a good distance from the other parents, so they were out of earshot. Rachel looks into Stan's eyes and begins, "Stan, there is something that I just realized recently." Rachel pulls out the 2004 photo and hands it to Stan. Stan squinches his eyes as he makes out the old Photo and sees himself and says, "Oh Wow! This brings back some memories. Wait, how do you have this?" Rachel replies, "In 2004, I was known as Angel." Stan looks at the picture again and sees her. He smiles and asks, "Angel with the Purple hair, right?" She responds, "Yeah, that was me."

Stan smiles big, saying, "Oh my gosh.. small world. Wow. I knew I recognized you. Well, this is a pleasant surprise." Rachel, with a straight face, says, "Is it?" Stans smile went to a grin as he said, "Occasionally… well, all right, often, ever since that trip, I would think about where you were, how you were doing and wondered why you skipped out on me." Rachel's head drops as she responds, "Yeah, about that. I wasn't ready for anything serious. Or so I thought. If it's any consolation, I ended up thinking about you from time to time as well." Surprised, Stan replies, "Really?" "But life had other plans for me," she said. Stan asks," What plans?" Rachel is having a hard time saying what she wants to say, so she tries a different approach. "Are you good at math, Stan?" she asks. Stunned, his reply was "Huh?" Now she was going to just do it. "Are you good at math? She asks. Stan replies, "Somewhat, I guess." Rachel goes on, "Ok, we're going to do a math equation." Stan says, "Ok."

She proceeds with the math lesson, "Take 2022 and subtract 2004. What do you get?" Stan does the subtraction in his head and answers, "Oh! It's eighteen." She nods her head and continues, "Yes, that's Right, Stan. Are you ready for the real Kicker? How old is Skyler?" Without missing a beat, he replies, "She's 18." Stan stops in his tracks after he speaks those words. There is a brief moment of uncomfortable silence as Rachel sees reality slap Stan in the face, and she says, "That's absolutely right, Stan.

Right then, the bell goes off, and he says, "Wait, so you're telling me that Skyler's my daughter?" Rachel responds, "Yes." Stan is stunned, but asks, "Does Skyler know?" Rachel replies, "No, I need you to keep it that way till you all get back. Then, we can all sit down together and talk. We don't need this to throw her off her game. Promise me." Stan agrees, "Ok, I promise."

Rachel smiles happily that he took the news well. "Thank you for not freaking out, but it just never seemed to be the right time to tell you." Stan takes a second, then speaks, "To be honest, now that I know, I wish we had crossed paths again years ago. Annie, when we get back, let's have dinner and talk more." Rachel smiles, tears in her eyes. "I would like that." They both head back to the group. Skyler wonders about what they are talking.

Coach rallies the team, "OK, everyone, are we ready to go to Sweden and then Europe?" Bodhi speaks up. "Coach, are you finally going to tell us why you had us add Sweden to the beginning of the trip?" Stan replies, "I forgot to feed my goldfish."

Logan shows Bodhi some pictures of Swedish girls on his phone. Bodhi's eyes grow wide. Bodhi says, "You know what, Coach, it doesn't matter; Stockholm it is." Bodhi gets a big hug from his mother, Kathy; Draven's mother, Brooke Pierce, gives Draven a big hug and a kiss. Logan's uncle says goodbye. Rachel says to Skyler, "Have a good time, and please listen to

Coach Ripley." Ripley, who still has a dumbfounded look on his face. Rachel adds, "Do what your coach tells you, ok? He's a good man." Skyler looks at her mother strangely and asks her, "You ok?" Rachel replies, "Yeah, have fun." Skyler kisses her mother and says, "Ok Mom, love you."

Zoe, Jett, and Lilly are hugging their parents. Tanner uses his strength to speak. "I am so proud of all of you. You are in good hands with Coach Ripley." All the kids hug the coach. Ripley takes control, "Ok, team, let's do this." The team heads to the dreaded TSA Line.

Chapter 29

FLIGHT 1973

The kids are bouncing with excitement. The kids walk in through the first-class seats. Jett says, "Sweet! 1st Class!" and attempts to take a seat. Stan grabs his Collar and guides him down the aisles, "Not today, Mr. Parker, keep moving." Jett responds, "You can't blame me for trying."

The kids buckle in their seats in the coach section, and the Flight Attendants start the safety spiel, "Welcome aboard, ladies and Gentlemen, this is Flight 1973 heading to Stockholm, Sweden."

Lilly is sitting with Draven, looking at a map, when she says, "First stop is Sweden, then Warsaw, Poland, then Slovakia, Vienna, Austria, Munich, Germany, Arlon, Belgium, London, and then back home to the States. I can't wait to show everyone all my passport stamps." Lilly looks at Draven and says, "You know, Draven, you're the 1st boy I ever went on a trip with, and we are going to Europe, of all places." Draven does a half smile. As we go down the aisle, we see Skyler and Jett sitting together. Skyler is looking off into space, and Jett tries to get her attention, "Hey... Earth to Skyler." She replies, "Sorry, just a lot going on at once." Jett replies, "Well, let's take this time to relax and sleep. It's going to be an exceptionally long flight. I hear Jet lag really sucks, so we need to sleep as much as we can because once we get there, it will be a roller coaster of a trip. Want to fall asleep to a movie like an old couple?" Jett asks. Skyler giggles and grabs a blanket, and says, "That sounds perfect."

The two of them cuddle under the blanket, watching an in-flight movie. Behind them are Logan and Bodhi, who are playing games on their phones. Across the aisle are Draven and Lilly. Lilly is talking about facts about the different countries they are going to. Behind them is Coach Ripley, who is having a grown-up drink. He is staring at the back of Skyler's seat with a perplexed look on his face. The picture that Rachel gave him was on his flight tray table. He looks back down and picks it up, staring as he grabs his glass and takes a drink. The Flight attendant walks by. And Stan gets her attention, "Excuse me, Ma'am. Would you be so kind as to bring me another? Make that two more. This is going to be an exceedingly long flight." The Flight attendant responds, "Yes, Sir, My pleasure." Stan looks at the Picture again and remembers.

1028 Publishing House © 2025

Inside a Belgian hotel bedroom in 2004, the closing of the front door awakens a young Stan with sand in his eyes. He rolls over to kiss Angel and sees she is gone. He drops his head in disappointment, then looks up and sees a sticky note on her pillow. It reads, "It's me, not you". Stan rolls back over, feeling defeated.

Back on the plane, Stan looks at Rachel in the picture, then puts it in his jacket. He looks down the aisle at Skyler, gives a little smile, and closes his eyes. We go back down the aisle. Passing the students and passengers who are sleeping.

The plane flies into the moonlight over Europe. We see a luxurious Castle in the mountains, Location unknown, with a full, bright moon behind it.

1028 Publishing House © 2025

Chapter 30

<u>FLYER X'S LAIR</u>

We see the interior of a large room inside a castle that looks like a museum to the art of flight and space. We see only the back of Flyer X as he removes a Black mask, puts it on a mask stand, grabs his black-tinted helmet, and puts it on. We never see his face. There are Pictures on the walls and on the shelves of Flyer X from around the world at Body Flight competitions, featuring notable celebrities and Royalty, but only with his helmet or mask on. We come to an oversized, handcrafted office Desk With one 8x10 framed image of a beautiful woman taken in the 90s. 2 large, oversized doors that were at least twenty feet high, open, and we see a butler walk in. He walks about fifty feet and tilts his head up towards a spiral staircase leading to the second floor. Flyer X is on the second floor, going through old Vinyl records. Searching for the perfect song. The butler inquires, "Sir... Sir..." Flyer X leans over the rail, looking at his butler with his helmet on. The butler asks, "Sir, do you want me to drive, Sir?" Flyer X nods his helmet with a thumbs up. The butler responds, "Very well, Sir. I will start the Engines."

1028 Publishing House © 2025

Flyer X continues thumbing through his record collection and finds the perfect song. He opens the player lid, places the vinyl on the center pin, and slowly lowers the needle onto the record. We see the butler grab a special key out of a wall cabinet with all the car and house keys. Next, we see the key put in the ignition, and a red light turns on. Pictures start shaking like in a minor earthquake, but with the roar and vibration of two massive engines. We see the Butler in a glass booth, sitting at the controls and watching the video monitors showing the rising wind speed. We catch a glimpse of the face of the Stoic Butler, who starts to Grin like a little boy. We see the gauges and monitors light up as the engines roar. As we pull back, we see that the butler has started the engines to Flyer X's very own personal three-story home Flight Chamber. As always, Flyer X is in his all-black suit with a large X across the chest, his tinted black helmet, and black boots with a custom grey X on the soles. Flyer X hits play and hustles down the spiral staircase, enters the flight chamber, and begins to do his routine to his music selection. The routine is Flawless. Three-quarters of the way through his song, we see a flashing red light in the room near the computer on his desk. The butler gestures to Flyer X, who is flying in the chamber. This was the important line that was ringing.

Flyer X hand gestures to his Butler to kill the engines. He floats down and flies out the door. Opens the sliding door to the main room and walks over to his desk. The red light keeps flashing till Flyer X hits a key on his keyboard. An encrypted chat window pops up. Flyer X reads the first message from "Orbital". It says, "They will be in Sweden in 18 hours". Flyer X responds, "And so will I". Flyer X closes the chat window. He turns and heads back to the chamber. The butler is waiting in the driver's seat. Flyer X twirls his finger in the air to say, Start the engines back up.

1028 Publishing House © 2025

Chapter 31

CREATING MEMORIES

The team arrives at the Downtown Camper in Stockholm. This hotel was designed for extreme sports enthusiasts and outdoor adventurers alike. The kids are excited as they walk up to the reception desk to be greeted in a foreign country for the first time. The receptionist greeted them, "Welcome back, Mr. Ripley." Stan responds, "Hello Tindra, it's good to be back. We have a reservation under the team's name, Wind Flyers. She checks her computer and says, "Yes sir, we have you down for eight guests, three rooms, and two nights with complimentary meals included." "Thank you, Tindra." Coach says. She responds, "So are these recruits?" Stan smiles and says, "This is my new team from the States, The Wind Flyers. They are getting their first taste of Europe." Looking at the kids, she says, "Be sure to listen to your coach. He is one of the best in the world. You should feel lucky to have him." Coach Ripley responds, "Thanks, Tindra." The girls look at the coach with a look, and he responds, "She and I used to wingsuit together." He turns back to Tindra, "Well, thank you, Tindra. Chat soon."

The team gets to floor and a long hallway. Coach hands out keys. "Ok, ladies, here is your room and your keys. Don't lose them. Here you go, boys, this is your room. I will be in the room here next door. Get unpacked, shower, clean up, and we will meet downstairs for dinner in 2 hours."

The kids enter their rooms. In the girls' room, they feel like princesses in a royal palace in Sweden. The boys run to the balcony and start looking at the view. Jett says, "This place is amazing." Logan chimes in, "I got first dibs on the shower." Bodhi shouts, "I call 2nd." Jett looks out at the world and takes a deep breath. Right then, we hear Logan echo in the bathroom, "No fricken way!" Logan runs back into the room, all excited, "Man, this place is so fancy that they even have a water fountain next to the toilet." Draven comments, "Dude, no way!" Draven runs into the bathroom to look for himself. We hear his echo in the bathroom, "Dude! You can release the toxins in your body and re-hydrate at the same time." He then returns to the room and says, "These Europeans are so sophisticated." Why don't we get water fountains in the bathroom? Man, we are so behind the times."

In the Third hotel room, Stan walks in, drops his bags, and turns on the TV. An American news broadcast, rebroadcasted with Swedish subtitles, is playing. It's Grace Monroe, the most trusted American woman on TV. She is loved around the world. Stan turns the volume up, and we hear Grace Monroe, who is in the middle of a rant, "Who is stealing sensitive Top-Secret Documents from Space labs from around the world? Authorities are frustrated and left with zero clues."

Stan picks up his jacket, pulls out the picture from Belgium, looks at it, and sets it on the bedside stand by the phone. His eyes slowly close, and the world fades to black.

We hear knocking on his hotel door and bad Swedish comedy blaring on the TV. He wakes up to the knocking and fumbles to find the remote to mute the TV. He had fallen asleep for 2 hours, and the kids were hungry.

Jett knocks on the door. "Coach, are you in there?" The door opens up, and a very tired Stan looks at the kids. Zoe asks, "Ready to get some grub, Coach?" With sand in his eyes, stan speaks, "Yeah, sorry, I passed out. Head down there, and I will be there in a few minutes. Jett affirms the plans, "Ok, coach." The team heads downstairs to the Buffet.

The kids are amazed by all the food and the many selections, and they begin to chow down.

Coach Ripley walks in, grabs a plate, and joins the kids at the table. They are all having a wonderful time and are stuffed with food. Coach Ripley asks everyone, "Did everyone get their fill?" Draven responds, "I think I ate a little of everything." Logan says, "And that was a lot." "Even for you," Lilly says. Skyler speaks up next, "So, Coach, you live here?" Stan answers, "That's right. Close to 2 years now." Skyler asks him, "So, what goes on at night in Sweden?" Smiling, Stan replies, "Well, Skyler, I'm glad you asked. Everyone, grab your coats and follow me, please." The kids all look at each other, grab their coats, and leave the table.

They head towards the hotel door and then outside. A tour bus of Swedish Female athletes who all look like they stepped off the covers of model magazines starts stepping off the bus. One by one, they pass the boys as they go into the hotel, smiling and saying hello in their Swedish accents. The boys are just melting as each girl passes by. When the last one walks by, Bodhi turns to follow the girls back into the hotel. Stan grabs Bodhi by the collar and whips him back around towards the outside. "Whoa there cowboy, we are going this way," Stan says. Bodhi responds, "But I think it would be a better idea if I went that way. I wouldn't be a gentleman (Grabbing Logan). I mean, we, we would not be gentlemen if we didn't at least introduce ourselves." Logan backs him up, "You know, coach, Bodhi has a point. We should say hello, being that we're representatives of the U.S. It would be a diplomatic thing to do." Jett gets the stink eye from Skyler, and she says, "Don't even think of joining that conversation." Jett laughs, saying, "I don't need to." Skyler smiles and says, "Good save, mister...I think I'll keep you around a little longer." Stan speaks, "Guys, I can see you are appreciating the new culture and all but also know there are all kinds of beauty."

Bodhi speaks up, "I couldn't agree more, coach, cause I just had a large variety of beauty walk right past us, acknowledging my existence; shoot, they even noticed Logan." Stan agrees, "O.K. Point taken. Oh, to be young ... Look, I wanted to bring you to Sweden so I could share something special with you all before we went to Europe. "What is it, coach?' Lilly asks. Stan replies, "Well, before I can tell you that, I need you to all trust me and close your eyes." The kids close their eyes. Stan continues, "Now, tilt your head up to the sky and open your eyes." The kids do what they're told and are stunned. They all open their eyes to see for the first time in their lives, the Aurora Borealis. The kids are nearly speechless. Jett speaks first, "This is unreal!" "It's so pretty," declares Lilly. Skyler looks at the coach and says, "Thank you, coach, for sharing this." "My pleasure, Skyler. Just wanted to create some memories for this trip." Lilly agrees, "That you did, Coach, and this is just our 1st night on this adventure."

The kids and Coach Ripley gaze up as the Arora dances across the night sky.

Chapter 32

<u>RIPLEY'S BIG SURPRISE</u>

Early the next morning, after a hearty breakfast, the team is in a taxi van driving through the city. The kids are taking in the sights. Zoe asks the coach, "So, Coach, what is all the mystery about today? Where are we going?" Coach Ripley responds to Zoe, "Well, since I didn't have a gift for Jett for his 18th Birthday and this is the only place like this in the world where we are going, I thought, why not take you guys to the next level of body flight? Today, Jett and the rest of you will learn the ways of the wingsuit at the world's only Wingsuit air chamber. So, to answer your question. This is why we came to Stockholm.

Jett is stoked, "I wish I could turn eighteen every year! This is awesome." Lilly Chimes in, "I thought you had to be 18 to do this." Coach Ripley responds, "Well, that's true in the real world, Lilly, and you can't skydive either. But this is a Wingsuit tunnel, and just like your tunnel back home, kids can do it too. So yes, you will get to do this today, too." The kids are pumped and have a full day of training on controlling their wingsuits.

1028 Publishing House © 2025

When they get to the tunnel, they see Flyer X in the Chamber in his all-black wingsuit training. Surprised, Lilly asks, "Is that Flyer X?" Jett, as well, is astonished to see Flyer X here. He replies, "It sure is. Coach, does Flyer X live here?" Puzzled as well, Coach Ripley says, "Not that I'm aware of." Jett asks, "Does he come here often?" "No, actually, this is the 1st time I have seen him here."

Flyer X finishes his flight time and walks out of the chamber door. He pulls his phone out of a pocket in his bag on a bench and checks his messages, never taking off his tinted shield helmet. The kids walk up to Flyer X. He sees the kids and starts typing on his translator. The phone translator app starts speaking in English: "Welcome to Stockholm Wind Flyers." Jett is flattered that Flyer X remembered them and asks, "Hey, Flyer X, what are you doing in Sweden?" Flyer X reads the translation on his phone and then types his response, "I'm training to fly the Crack in Switzerland." With curiosity, Jett asks Flyer X, "The Crack? What's that?" Coach Ripley jumps in to answer the question, "One of the most dangerous flight paths in the world for wingsuit flyers." Flyer X makes a gesture to say, BINGO. Coach Ripley continues, "It's a flight path for the pros. Not for newbies. Well, Mr. X, it was nice to finally meet you, but time is short, and I have to get this team in the chamber." Flyer X shakes everyone's hands, then puts his arm over his chest and gives them a little bow, grabs his bag, and leaves. As he leaves, people are asking for selfies and autographs as he walks out.

Jett asks the question, "Do you think anyone knows who Flyer X is?" Bodhi replies, "He is an enigma."

The kids head to the chamber and take turns flying as Stan trains them.

In the wind tunnel, Stan and other trainers at the facility work with each kid, teaching them the art of wingsuit flying.

Later that day, the team is taking a break, and Lilly makes a suggestion, "Can we make a deal? When I turn eighteen, can we all plan a trip to do this for real together?" Jett says, "That sounds feasible, sis."

After a full day of training, the team is back at the hotel having dinner. Coach Ripley addresses his team, "I'm glad you enjoyed today. Tomorrow we have an early flight to Warsaw, so no staying up or sleeping in. I want to see all your bags packed up and by the door before you go to bed tonight. Warning: I will be pounding on your doors at exactly 7 am to take you all down for breakfast. Any questions? No? Good. I'll see you all in the morning." Everyone says good night, and they all go into their rooms.

Chapter 33

<u>WARSAW, POLAND</u>

The kids get into a Taxi Van and head to the event. Jett says, "I can't believe we are actually doing this." Skyler leans into him and reminds him, "Well, this was all your idea, remember?" Jett knows this, but it all feels surreal to him: "Yeah, it's just wild that we have made it." Coach Ripley interrupts them and says, "Ok, team, this is our first competition. Let's stay focused and have a good time while we are in Europe." The kids get out of the Taxi Van and head to the front door.

The kids enter Fly Spot, Warsaw's own Wind Tunnel. Competitions have already begun, and we see flyers competing in the chamber. The team finds an area with seats, claims it, and begins pulling out their gear to change. Looking around, Skyler says, "Well, this is a lot different than back home." Coach Ripley responds, "That's because you all have now gone international. Welcome to the big leagues." Draven gives his input, "This is pretty awesome."

As flyers from around the world walk by, they introduce and welcome the Wind Flyers. The female British team walks up to them. A British

1028 Publishing House © 2025

female with dark hair, in her British Accent, introduces herself and her team, "Hi, I'm Dalea. We're the British team. We haven't seen you on the circuit before." Skyler is so happy to meet so many other female flyers from around the world. She puts her hand out and says with a smile, "Hi, I'm Skyler, and we are Team Wind Flyers." Dalea's first question is, "Americans?" Bodhi stumbles to get up to be recognized, "Yes, yes, Ma'am, we are. Hi, I'm Bodhi, and this is Draven, Lilly, Zoe, and Jett. You met Skyler, and this is Coach Ripley."

Dalea continues with the introductions, "Well, nice to meet you. These are Tabitha, Jennifer, Stacey, & Crystal. Welcome to Poland. We look forward to seeing you in the chamber." Bodhi is starting to blush, "Thanks. We look forward to seeing you as well." He said. Dalea then asks, "Will you all be at the competition in London?" Bodhi responds, "That's our plan, Ma'am." The British team giggles, and Dalea says, "Ma'am? How proper. I just love your accent, Bodhi. We'll see you around."

Bodhi is Giddy as they walk away. He leans over to Skyler, "Skyler, you were right. I will never doubt you again. The women here are like from another world."

1028 Publishing House © 2025

The announcer comes on the speaker, "Next up is Draven Pierce." Draven walks up to the chamber entrance. His team and the audience are cheering him on. He cues the music, enters the chamber, and begins his routine. The music is pumping, and the crowd is getting into the performance. The announcer continues, "This is Draven Pierce's 1st competition, along with his team, the Wind Flyers from Pinetop-Lakeside, Arizona, U.S.A."

Bodhi finishes his routine with high marks. He comes back over to his team, who are congratulating him. Coach Ripley congratulates Draven, "Good Job, Draven!"

Some female flyers from Brazil look over at Draven, smiling and giving him a thumbs up. Draven starts to blush. "I think I want to move to Europe." He says. Logan corrects him, "I think they're from Brazil." And with a stink eye, Lilly looks at Draven and says, "Seriously?"

The event announcer calls the next flyer, "Next up is Skyler Jenkins from the United States." Skyler, in her all-white suit and helmet, closes her visor. The music starts, and Skyler does what she does best and wows the crowd. She finishes with High marks.

1028 Publishing House © 2025

The team is cheering her on as she comes back to the table. Coach gives his accolades, "Excellent, Skyler. Now, just keep that momentum going the rest of the trip."

Zoe looks over at the holding area, sees Leonid Volkov, and is starstruck. "Oh my God, look!" she says. Zoe points over to the holding area at Leonid. "It's Leonid Volkov!" she squeals. The kids are star-struck, but Jett looks worried. Coach notices and reassures Jett, "Jett, you will do fine. Don't let him being here mess with your focus." "Worried?" Jett says, "But it's Leonid Volkov, the 3-time world Champion." Jett starts to panic. Coach Ripley tries to stop this before it gets worse and says to Jett, "Jett, close your eyes and take a deep, slow breath. You got this, Jett. Remember, you have your secret weapon. No one does what you do. Not even Volkov"

The announcer gets back on the microphone, "Here is a 3-time World Champion from St. Petersburg, Russia, a true showman, Leonid Volkov." The crowd gets loud, knowing they are in for a show.

Leonid's music begins, and the superstar enters the chamber, his movements controlled with pristine precision. The audience is in awe of his control of his body. His control in the air is mind-boggling. He finishes, and the crowd cheers.

The announcer gets back on the microphone, "What an amazing performance of control and skill from Leonid Volkov. Now from the United States, for his very first chamber flight in Europe, here is Jett Parker." Jett walks into the holding area and passes Leonid. Leonid stops him and says, "So, you're Jett Parker?" Jett is flabbergasted that Leonid knew his name. Tongue-tied, Jett does his best to respond, "Yes, Hi, I'm Jett Parker." Leonid replies, "Dah!" Jett stares at Leonid for a moment too long, and it gets awkward, so Jett gets back into the conversation with some flattery: "You were amazing in there." Leonid, with a serious Russian look on his face, replies, "Thank you. Now, it is you I wish to see in the Chamber. So, let's see what you got."

The crowd cheers, and the music begins. Jett enters the chamber and begins his routine. The crowd is astonished when he incorporates his secret parkour moves, rolls multiple times, and leaps off the glass tube from side to side, as if he is jumping from building to building. Leonid is impressed. The crowd is up on their feet, cheering as they witness this new element to the sport. The song ends, and Jett waves to the audience and heads back to the team table.

The Crowd goes wild. Every team from around the world is blown away by what they witnessed. The team congratulates Jett on his performance as he comes back to the table. The judges put up high scores. We see Leonid smiling and clapping for Jett. Leonid walks over to the team table and congratulates him. The team is giddy as he approaches them, especially Zoe and Lilly, who have dreamy eyes for Leonid as he speaks with his Russian Accent.

Leonid looks right at Jett and gives a slight grin. "Very impressive, Mr. Parker." Jett's head is spinning with just that small compliment from such a world-class flyer. "Thank you," Jett says. Leonid then asks, "So, this is your Coach?" Ripley, proud to meet Leonid, says, "Hello Leonid, it is an honor to meet you. I'm Coach Ripley." Leonid replies, "The honor is all mine, Coach Ripley. Where did you come up with those unique moves?" Like a proud dad, Coach Ripley says, "Those were all Jett's moves, actually." Leonid is now more intrigued than ever. "Really?" Leonid asks. Coach adds, "He used to do Parkour." Leonid asks, "What is Parkour?" Jett replies, "Free running."

1028 Publishing House © 2025

Now that it's clarified what Parkour was, Leonid says, "Ah, yes, that's where people jump off buildings and walls, correct?" Jett answers, "Yes. I used to do Free Running with a crew when I lived in Dallas, Texas." Leonid's eyes light up, "So you are from Texas? I love the show Dallas. Who shot J.R.? And America's Team, Go Cowboys! Bodhi Chimes in, "I love their Cheerleaders." Leonid smiles with a laugh, " Who doesn't? Dah." They make the game much, much better."

"It was so nice to meet all of you, but I must go now. Some of my students are competing, and I must be with them now, but let's have a discussion later, you and I, Mr. Parker." Jett responds, "Dah!" Leonid laughs, "Dah! Yes, you learn quickly, Mr. Parker. It was nice to meet you all. Good luck today." The kids say goodbye, and the girls have dreamy eyes as he walks away.

The Competitions are over, and the announcer begins to announce the winners. Skyler and Jett finish 2nd and 3rd, respectively, and Leonid wins first place. On the winner's steps, Leonid leans over to Jett and says respectfully and smiling with his trophy, "It's been a while since I felt worried about competition. But I welcome it. I am Glad you are on the Circuit this year, Mr.

Parker. It will keep things interesting." Jett smiles as if he were given the best compliment.

1028 Publishing House © 2025

Chapter 34

<u>IN THE BIG LEAGUES NOW</u>

At the world-famous Hurricane Factory in Slovakia, the team keeps up and holds their own; celeb flyers that the kids grew up emulating were all here. It's another day of competitions, and the team is ripping it up in the chamber, wowing the crowd. The next thing we see is the winners' steps, with Lilly and Skyler in 2nd and 3rd place. As the crowd cheers, we see on the flat-screen TVs at the bar that a local news broadcast is reporting on the theft of classified documents from the Institute for Experimental Physics in Kosice. Authorities are currently looking for the suspect. No one seems to notice it.

It's dark, and the team is catching some sleep on the tour bus as they cross over into Austria, headed to Vienna. The bus passes the Vienna Aerospace Laboratory. It is after hours. In the Laboratory parking lot, we see an aerospace lab building and hear an alarm system going off. Lights around the building are flashing or strobing. Running into the parking lot is a man in all black, carrying a backpack and wearing a mask, heading toward a black 2023 BMW F850 GS Motorcycle. He jumps on and takes off as security comes running out of the building, chasing him. They are yelling on the radio, giving his description.

We see the suspect in all black racing through the streets of Vienna. He passes a police vehicle that turns on its lights and pursues. Multiple Police cars join in the pursuit.

Onboard the tour bus, everyone is sleeping until they are all woken by multiple police sirens. The team wakes up and looks out their windows, seeing a black motorcycle zoom past the tour bus, with police in close pursuit. Draven comments, "Damn! Someone is in trouble." The bus driver gets on the intercom and announces, "We will be at the hotel in 20 minutes."

In their Vienna Hotel room, Jett and the boys are getting ready for bed when they notice police helicopters with search lights scouring the area for the suspect. Draven walks to the balcony window and says, "Do you think they are still looking for the guy on the motorcycle? Jett replies, maybe. Turn on the News and see if they are covering it.

Bodhi turns on the news. They have a live feed from one of the news helicopters. Everything is spoken in the native language, and the boys are doing their best to understand what they are saying. The helicopter is doing its best to find the suspect but fails. Jett announces, "Oh well, I got 1st dibs on the shower."

The next morning, the team was at it again. This time, it was Windobana Indoor Skydiving in Vienna. We see the team and other celeb flyers. Once again, flyers from around the world gather for another day of exciting competitions. Flyer X walks into the room, and the crowd swarms to him, taking pictures. He stands perfectly still as people go to him for selfies. He stands stoic without emotion. Jett and the team watch from across the room. We see small cameos of well-known flyers performing in the chamber. We see other teams in the practice rooms rolling around on crawlers, going over routines. Sports anchors are streaming live from their booths, interviewing flyers. We see that these athletes are not just competitors but friends who lift each other up. We see them share suggestions. There is no hate or ill will toward others, as you would see at most sporting events. The Wind Flyers are gathered together in their area, and the coach walks up.

Coach Ripley addresses the team. "Believe it or not, we are halfway through this trip. And you guys have been awesome." Jett points out something, "Did you see Flyer X is here?"

Coach replies, "Yeah, it was hard not to notice. You would think he was a rock star or something." Zoe, with her eyes focused on Flyer X, "He is a master of Marketing, and we all eat it up." She says. Lilly chimes in, "You have to love his charisma, though."

Throughout the day, we see various team members, Flyer X, Leonid Volkov, and others, make stunning moves to killer music. We see multiple winners, including Leonid in 1st and Jett in third, as well as Lilly in 2nd and Draven in third. We also see team winners from different countries.

Back in the States, in Lakeside, we see Family and Friends watching the competition via livestream at the Parker House. Annie brings out snacks and sits next to Tanner in his wheelchair, cheering them on.

Back at the competition, we see the team celebrating at the outdoor awards banquet next to their on-site theme park, meeting new flyers. Jett is with his team, speaking with the Belgium Team, when Leonid walks up to Jett and says, "Mr. Parker, do you have a moment? We didn't get a chance to speak in Warsaw. I figured now might suffice." Jett stops what he's doing and excuses himself from the group, "Of course. Excuse me,

1028 Publishing House © 2025

everyone. If I don't see you again tonight, I will see you all at Luxfly. Bonsoir!" The Belgian team responds "Bonsoir!" Leonid and Jett walk away. Leonid starts, "Mr. Parker." stops him and says, "You can just call me Jett. My Dad is Mr. Parker." Leonid replies, "And you can call me Leo." Jett smiles and says, "Cool." Leo asks, "Would you be interested in teaching one day, Jett?" Jett responds, "What do you mean? Teach indoor ?" Leo says, "I am not only a World Champion, but also teach flyers from around the world. I create my own training program and music. I do a lot of things... What I'm trying to say is, would you be interested in teaching this new form of yours to others?... Think about it. Making your mark and winning trophies is one thing. But seeing up-and-coming flyers use your moves and make them their own can be more fulfilling than a trophy. Knowing that you inspired someone to be better, in my opinion, is better than any prize. You still get paid and get to travel." Jett is amazed at what he is hearing. "Wow, you think I'm that good?" Jett asks. "Dah, You Have unique moves, yes. Anyone can improve... here is my card with email. Let's keep in touch." Leo says. Jett replies, "Dah."

Leonid gives Jett a Strong Russian Handshake and returns to the party. Lilly, Zoe, and Skyler approach Jett as he puts the card in his

1028 Publishing House © 2025

pocket. Lilly runs up to Jett, "OMG, what did he say, Jett?" Zoe jumps in, "Did he mention if he was single?" Skyler walks up and asks, "What did he say?" Jett is still wrapping his head around what happened and said, "He is not what I was expecting. I was expecting Dolph Lundgren from Rocky IV, but he turned out to be the complete opposite—a really nice guy. He might be my 1st Russian friend." Zoe interrupts, "That's great, Jett, but is he single?" Jett replies, "You should ask him next time we see him."

The team is on a 5-hour bus ride, taking in the sights as they drive from Vienna along the Austrian Alps to the Fly Station in Munich, Germany.

Chapter 35

<u>WHO IS ORBITAL?</u>

30,000 Feet in the air, Flyer X is sitting in his private jet, flying over Germany, looking at his laptop. A secure chat window pops up. We see the blinking icon begin to type a text message from Orbital.

ORBITAL-

Report...

FLYER X-

Everything is going as planned.

ORBITAL-

Is he suspicious?

FLYER X-

No. Has no reason to be.

ORBITAL-

Good. Keep me updated.

FLYER X-

Will do.

1028 Publishing House © 2025

In a Private, secure hangar at Munich International Airport. We see Flyer X's Black Jet pull into a private hangar. Two Limo SUVs are parked with a Security detail nearby. A Tall, Attractive British female in black business attire approaches the jet. The door opens, and Flyer X steps out in black pants, a black shirt, a black leather jacket with a dark grey X across it, and a black mask. She begins to brief him, "Welcome back, sir. Here is your intel: your villa and car keys are in the Garage. Security will transport you there now. You will be at the Fly Station Munich tomorrow at 10 am. The address is on your phone. Good luck, Sir." Flyer X, with his mask, nods yes, gets into the SUV, and they drive away.

A Black 2023 M8 Competition Coupe with tinted windows pulls up to the Front door of a large German Castle.. The valet opens the driver's door, and a man dressed in an expensive tuxedo gets out. He is wearing a black porcelain mask with a single upside-down heart painted under one eye, looking like a teardrop. He steps out, handing over the keys to the Valet. He walks up the red-carpeted stairs and into the castle doors.

Once inside, the mystery man walks into a large Masquerade ballroom. Everyone is masked and in small groups, talking. Music is playing, and

1028 Publishing House © 2025

some are dancing. A German woman across the room sees the mystery man and his teardrop. She walks over to him and says, "I was wondering if you would like to dance since you look, so sad?"

The masked man puts out his hand. She takes it, and he leads her to the dance floor. As they dance, she says to him, "Do you see that man over there trying to seem important? He is the head of Research and Development at ZD Space Agency. His laptop mysteriously duplicated itself last night while I held his attention." He twirls her out, then back into him and down to a dip. She looks into his eyes and says, "Your file did say you were the Strong, silent type." He brings her back up close, and she whispers, "It's in your pocket." He spins her round and then bows. He leaves the dance floor and goes out to the front to retrieve his car from the valet.

Chapter 36

MUNICH & BELGIUM & LONDON, OH MY!

Competitions go through the day, with all the main players. We see amazing performances. Then we see the team in their uniforms and helmets taking photos for airline marketing in exchange for plane tickets.

Another day of competitions for the team. Family and friends back home are watching on their phones and laptops, cheering them on. Others are rallying at the local steakhouse, watching on the Television sets, and cheering them on as they represent the United States.

The team is on a bus passing Big Ben. They are taking pics, soaking it all in. The bus pulls up to iFly Basingstoke in London, England. The kids get their stuff off the bus and walk into their final competitions, already making new friends.

Bodhi and Draven set their bags down and started unpacking their gear. Right then, Dalea and her teammates walk up to the boys, surprising them. "Hey, it's Bodhi, right?" Dalea asks. Bohdi responds, "Yes, Ma'am!" Dalea turns to her teammates, "Don't you just love how he says that?" Bodhi blushes. Dalea continues, "Would you like to keep in contact?" Bohdi's eyes light up, "Of course!" Dalea smiles big and says, "Excellent. This is my email and social media. Don't be a stranger. Bye."

They walk away, and Bodhi is on cloud nine, saying, "Dreams do come true." Coach Ripley intervenes, "Ok, Romeo, don't get hazy today. This is the final day, so let's show them what you got."

It's the final day, and the team is not holding back. Flyer X does all he can to keep his numbers high, and so does Leonid. But in the end, Jett beats Leonid and Flyer X. Multiple awards are given out for different categories, and the team goes home with a handful of awards.

Leonid congratulates Jett and his team, "Well, Jett, this was an exciting week. I have enjoyed the competition. Please consider my offer." Jett replies, "I will, Leo." If you come to St. Petersburg, how do you say? Hit me up, and we can go flying." Leo says. Jett answers, "Sounds like a plan." "Till then. Take care, Wind Flyers." The team says farewell and gathers up their things. Flyer X walks up to the team. With confidence, Zoe speaks up, "Hey, Flyer X."

Flyer X waves, walks over, and then uses his phone to translate. "You were all very impressive this season. I look forward to seeing more from you in the future. Jett, I have a feeling we will see each other again soon." Jett replies, "That would be great." Flyer X gestures to the coach and the team to squeeze together for a selfie. They crowd together, and Flyer X snaps the pic.

Chapter 37

<u>BACK HOME TO SURPRISES</u>

Family and friends wait as the team steps off a small plane and passes through the TSA checkpoint. Once they march through the doors, the family, and friends cheer as they walk in, showering hugs. Skyler is hugging Rachel and asks, "Well, how was it?" "It was amazing," Skyler said, "And I want to go back with you, OK?" Rachel smiles and looks over to Stan, who is off to the side by himself. Rachel hand gestures for him to come over. He walks over to Rachel and Skyler. Rachel says, "Hey, Coach." Stan replies with a smile, "Hello, Rachel." Rachel continues, "I just want to say thank you for taking care of Skyler for me." Stan responds, "It was my pleasure. She was amazing, you should have seen her." "Oh, I did! We all did." She said, "We followed you all, the whole way, via Livestreams. The whole mountain is talking about it. The Local paper wants to interview all of you." "Really, wow!" Skyler says. Rachel tells them both, "So, I would like to take you both out to dinner. We have a lot to discuss." Rachel looks at Stan. Stan realizes the time has finally come. They walk over to the team, which is surrounding Annie and Coach McAdams.

1028 Publishing House © 2025

Annie is giddy and can't hold it in anymore. "As you know, when Tanner collapsed, he was about to say something and never got to it until a few days ago." Jett, Lilly, Zoe, and the rest of the group are waiting with anticipation. Annie continues, "Two days ago, after a productive therapy session, he finished what he wanted to say. Tell them, Tanner." With a half smile filled with pride, Tanner says," I said, Annie Parker, will you marry me?" Lilly speaks up, "And what did you say, Mom?" Screaming, she said, "I said yes!" showing her ring. Everyone congratulates them as she shows off the ring.

Zoe leans into Jett and says, "What did I tell you, Jett?" Jett concedes, "You were right... Sis." Zoe smiles.

Chapter 38

<u>THE BIG DAY</u>

It's finally here, Graduation Day for the class of 2023, and students are crossing the stage to get their diplomas. We see Bodhi and Logan about to ham it up for the crowd as they come up the stairs when they see their mothers, Brooke, and Kathy, looking at them with the Mom Eye, and they snap back into line to properly receive their Diplomas. Skyler follows, and then Jett. Coach McAdams, Annie, Lilly, and Zoe are all together like a proud family. Rachel and Stan are standing next to them, proud of their girl as well. At that moment, a Uniformed Planetary Defense Officer walks up to Jett and Skyler. "Excuse me, Sir, you are Jett Parker and Skyler Jenkins, are you not?" He says. Jett responds, "Yes, that would be us." The Planetary Defense Officer hands Jett a package and says, "I was given orders by General Parker himself to personally hand-deliver these to you both. He also asked me to convey his deepest apologies for not being able to attend today's festivities and that he will make it up to you and see you soon." The officer hands them both envelopes and walks away.

1028 Publishing House © 2025

Jett is confused and asks Skyler, "Why did you get one?" "I went to the recruitment office." She said.

They both look at each other and smile. They tear open the envelopes and discover that they have both been accepted as recruits and will be a part of the Planetary Defense Force, starting in 6 months. Everyone is happy for the two of them.

1028 Publishing House © 2025

Chapter 39

<u>THE CHANCE OF A LIFETIME</u>

Jett is just finishing up with some students in the practice room at iFly. Skyler comes in and takes over. Jett heads over to the counter to start filling out the students' certificates. Zoe walks in, going through a stack of mail, reading what they got, "Bills, Bills, Junk, Bills. Huh? Hey Jett." Jett replies, "Ya Sis." Zoe continues, "There is a fancy letter here for you." Jett is handed the envelope, and he asks, "For me?" Jett takes the envelope and sees his name on the front, but no return address. He flips it over and sees what appears to be a royal wax seal. It says WEBSTER CASTLE around the edge of the ring, and in the middle, a large X. Jett gets a letter opener and slices the top of the envelope. He gently pulls out an expensive parchment card and reads it. "I am sorry I could not be there for your right of passage, Jett. I hope this gift will make up for it. Here is your plane ticket. When you reach your destination, ask Mia to point you over to Hangar 28. When you get there, ask for Yves Rossey. I thought you would enjoy this excursion before you go into the service. Enjoy, X." Jett is stunned. The ticket is a week from today for a private Jet, destination unknown.

It's a week later, and Jett walks up to the Black Jet and a British Flight Attendant, who turns out to be the same woman we saw in Munich. She welcomes Jett on board the plane. "Welcome aboard, Mr. Parker. My name is Mia, and I will be your flight attendant for this trip." "Hello, Mia," Jett says. Jet sits down, and Mia offers him a refreshment. "I know this might be a strange question, being that I'm already on the plane, but where exactly am I going?" Jett kindly asks. Mia smiles and reassures Jett, "You are in good hands, Mr. Parker. It will be worth the wait." Jett asks, "Can you at least tell me how long the flight is?" Mia responds, "That, I can reveal Mr. Parker. Today's flight time will be 15 hours and 22 minutes, weather permitting. So, buckle up, Mr. Parker, because you're in for one heck of a ride."

We see Jett sheepishly giving a little smirk. The music kicks in on his EarPods, and Jett drifts off to sleep.

Jett wakes up in the morning, with the sun beaming through the plane window as it comes in for a landing. The captain comes on the cabin speakers. "Good morning, Mr. Parker. I hope you got some rest. I just wanted to be the first to welcome you to Paris." Jett is shocked, "Paris!"

1028 Publishing House © 2025

Mia, with a gorgeous smile, says, "Yes, Mr. Parker, Paris, France."

Jett walks off the plane. Mia says, "Have a great time, Mr. Parker. We will see you on the trip back." Jett feels blessed, "Wonderful, thank you, Mia. Oh ya, do you know where Hangar 28 is?" Mia points him in the direction. Jett grabs his bag and walks over to hangar twenty-eight. The large hangar door is open halfway with a Black helicopter outside. An older man is working on some components.

Jett says, "Hello!" The older man turns towards Jett, looks him up and down, and says, "Hello... American?" Jett responds, "Yes, my name is Jett Parker, and I'm supposed to find someone named Yves." Yves puts down his tools, grabs a rag, and wipes his hands to shake hands with Jett. He says, "Ah, so you're Jett Parker. Flyer X said you were coming. He said that you were an Adrenaline junkie." Jett replies, "I guess you could say that. So, you know Flyer X?" Yves answers, "Yes, for many years now." Jett asks, "So who is he?" Yves replies, "That is an exceptionally good question. That will be answered in due course. Until then, are you interested in taking your thrill to another level?" Jett answers with "Always."

Chapter 40

A LEAP OF FAITH

A killer music track comes in hard through Jett's EarPods, and we see Jett's eyes wide in his helmet as he looks across to Yves, who is hanging on the other side of the helicopter with a wing foil strapped to his back. We then see that Jett, too, has a wing foil on his back. Yves holds up his hand and counts down from 3, 2, 1. Sweat beads down Jett's face, and they both lean back and fall from both sides of the helicopter. They both fall towards the earth, then start their jet engines and shoot back up into the sky. We see Jett's face glowing with excitement like never before, and all he can do is yell, "Yahoo!"

Jett comes blazing, straight towards you, the reader, then, taking a hard right, flies out of sight.

THE END

Stay tuned, Jett Parker returns in the third installment of the FLY Series.

FLY

ORBITAL CONTROL

www.ingramcontent.com/pod-product-compliance
Lightning Source LLC
Chambersburg PA
CBHW060117260626
47160CB00005B/1911